FR...
NANCY DREW FILES

THE CASE: Foul play destroys the fun and games at Club High Adventure.

CONTACT: Marva Phillips, owner of the club, has always loved to take risks—but the odds have been in her favor, until now.

SUSPECTS: Roger Coleman—the ruthless young businessman is determined to take control of the club, whatever the price.

Al Hunt—the rock-climbing instructor is ready to help Nancy in any way he can, except by answering questions about his own past.

Gil Forrest—Marva's handsome fiancé keeps a close eye on her finances—and on her prettiest young students.

Sara Lakin—she has a desperate crush on Gil, and she'll crush anyone who stands in her way.

COMPLICATIONS: While Nancy is flirting with danger, Gil Forrest is flirting with her.

Books in The Nancy Drew Files™ Series

Available from ARCHWAY Paperbacks

THE NANCY DREW FILES™ CASE ■ 36

OVER THE EDGE

Carolyn Keene

AN ARCHWAY PAPERBACK
Published by POCKET BOOKS
New York   London   Toronto   Sydney   Tokyo

AN ARCHWAY PAPERBACK *Original*

An Archway Paperback published by
POCKET BOOKS, a division of Simon & Schuster Inc.
1230 Avenue of the Americas, New York, NY 10020

ISBN: 0-671-64703-2

First Archway Paperback printing June 1989

10 9 8 7 6 5 4 3 2 1

OVER
THE EDGE

Chapter

One

"Nancy, watch where you're going!" With a shudder, Bess Marvin glanced at the waves dashing against the rocks below the cliff road and squeezed her eyes shut. "You're going to get us killed."

Nancy Drew, hands competently gripping the wheel of the rented jeep, shot a quick look at her friend. "Calm down, Bess," she called into the sea breeze that was blowing her hair back from her face into a red-gold halo. "I'm in complete control."

"Yeah, come on, Bess," George Fayne said from the backseat. "Relax." Leaning forward, she touched her cousin Bess's arm. "Open

1

your eyes. The Oregon coast is one of the most beautiful in the world, and you're missing it."

Bess just shook her head and yanked her floppy khaki hat down over her eyes. She slid even lower in her seat. "If we're going to die, I don't want to watch it happening."

"Sometimes I don't understand you," George said, shaking her head. "Only a couple of hours ago we were in a plane that was five miles up in the air. You weren't scared then. But now you're terrified because we happen to be a few hundred feet above the ocean waves."

"And rocks—don't forget the rocks," Nancy teased.

"Stop it, you two," Bess wailed. "You're not being fair. Anyway, a plane's different. You're closed in, in a nice comfy seat, with someone bringing you food—" She paused to sigh, a smile on her face. "That cabin attendant was adorable, wasn't he?"

"Now, that's the Bess I know and love." George grinned.

George caught Nancy's eye in the rearview mirror, and they exchanged knowing smiles. Bess could be on an arctic iceberg and still manage to find a cute guy.

George and Bess were cousins as well as best friends, but they were complete opposites. George had short, curly dark hair, dark eyes, and the long, toned body of an athlete. Bess was blond with a short, curvy body and a two-track mind—boys and food.

"Okay, I'll admit this is a fairly gorgeous place," Bess said, forgetting her fears long enough to raise the brim of her hat and peer around. "But I'll still be glad to get off this road. How much farther to Club High Adventure?" Then she added with a low mutter, "As if we need more adventure after this!"

"Not too far," Nancy assured her.

"Hey," George said, "for a few minutes there I almost forgot we're here on a case." She made a sweeping motion toward the pine- and alder-covered hills that rose sharply to the left of their jeep. "I was only thinking about getting on my hiking boots and tackling these mountains."

Bess glanced at Nancy with a small, worried frown. "Do you think it's going to be a dangerous case?"

"It doesn't sound all that serious. And it'll probably take only a day or two to clear up." Then she laughed. "But how many times have I said that, and then it's turned out to be just the opposite?"

At the age of eighteen, Nancy had established herself as a world-class detective. As the daughter of a well-known criminal attorney, Carson Drew, Nancy received many cases through her father. This one at Club High Adventure was no exception.

Marva Phillips, the daughter of an old college friend of Mr. Drew, had called him about the problems she was having with the club she had inherited at her father's death three years ago. Mr. Drew suggested that Nancy was just the person to help find a solution to the death threats Marva's guests had been receiving.

Although no real attempt had been made against anyone, Marva was afraid that her business would be ruined. On the phone she pointed out to Nancy that there wasn't a guest in the world who would voluntarily visit a resort where there was the possibility of being killed.

Nancy had agreed that the sooner she got to Oregon, the better. So after some hurried packing, Nancy, Bess, and George had boarded a plane to Portland, Oregon.

"Well, I sure hope we can find out who's sending the threats and fast," George said. "That way we'll have time to enjoy ourselves. Just looking at that brochure Marva sent you makes me drool. A resort totally devoted to wilderness sports, like rock climbing and kayaking and spelunking—" She closed her eyes and leaned back. "Now, that's my idea of heaven."

"I'll tell you what activity I think sounds like heaven," Bess piped up, checking her windblown hair with the aid of a pocket mirror.

"The evening barbecues with dancing under the stars." She cocked her head to one side. "Do you suppose they have a cute dancing instructor?" She shook her head at her own question. "Never mind. I'll find someone. Maybe a personal trainer. I'm glad I brought my new striped leotard—"

"I don't mean to interrupt," Nancy said, laughing. "But do either of you see a sign?" Nancy had downshifted and slowed the jeep to almost a crawl. The high hills to their left had fallen off into a thickly wooded ravine. "Marva said there'd be a sign to mark the entrance. But I don't see a space even wide enough to be called a driveway."

As they rounded the next bend, Bess pointed excitedly. The sign read: "Entrance to Club High Adventure." Nancy smiled and turned the jeep onto a narrow lane.

The gravel road climbed through a series of tight turns. Lush walls of overhanging trees on either side almost blocked out the sunlight. At ground level and nearly choking the road, light green ferns mixed with rich, dark rhododendrons, whose branches were almost solid with huge pink flowers. Nancy had to shift the jeep down to first.

"Talk about a wilderness getaway," Bess commented. "I almost expect to see Big Foot jump out from behind a rhododendron."

"You never know," George said. "This is the northwest. And if there really is a Big Foot, this is his stomping ground."

"Thanks. I really needed that." Bess groaned at George's joke. "How much farther, Nan?"

"Not too far, I hope. I'm glad we went for the four-wheel drive," Nancy said as their jeep bumped along the narrow gravel road.

"Yeah," George said. "We'd never make it if we'd listened to Bess and rented that red sports—" She broke off as they took the last steep turn. Suddenly they were out of the woods and at the top of the cliff.

Ahead of them lay a gentle sloping meadow, in the middle of which sat a cluster of buildings. Rising behind these were steps of increasingly taller hills, which finally led up to the high coastal mountains.

"That must be the main lodge," Nancy said, stopping the jeep long enough to take in her surroundings. She was pointing to a long, low contemporary structure of redwood and glass that sat at the edge of a sparkling crater lake. There were three small sailboats on the water, tacking into the breeze.

"Hmmm—that looks great," George said, watching the boats. "And it's one sport where I don't need lessons."

"Yeah," said Bess with a snort. "Along with karate, deep-sea diving, bicycling— Hey, check that out," she exclaimed. She was pointing almost directly overhead. "What kind of kite is that? It's huge."

Nancy stopped the jeep. The three girls hopped out and looked up to see a large yellow kitelike object floating above them.

"It isn't a kite, Bess," George said when she got a good look. "It's a hang glider. See, there's the pilot."

The glider had circled so that now they could see a white-helmeted figure hanging below the glider's sail. The pilot was holding onto a bar similar to that on a trapeze.

"That's the control bar," George explained, pointing.

"Now, that's something I'd really like to learn how to do," Nancy said with enthusiasm.

"Definitely," George agreed.

"What's definite," Bess said with a shudder, "is that you two are insane if you want to try anything that dangerous."

"Aw, come on, Bess," George coaxed. "Nothing could be better than flying on your own steam."

"You know what my idea of fun is," Bess retorted. "A pool, a bronzed hunk, and— Hey, that's pretty weird, the way that guy's flying that thing. What's he doing, anyway?"

"I don't know. Maybe some new kind of maneuver." George was frowning.

The glider had stopped making its wide, lazy

circles, and was instead stuttering with short jerks in midair. All at once, the yellow material began to ripple and then flap in the wind, as the glider rocked back and forth.

"Nancy!" George grabbed her friend's arm. "Doesn't it look like that guy's in trouble?"

As she spoke they watched the pilot frantically maneuvering the control bar, first pushing, then—apparently realizing that was the wrong move—pulling it back against himself. As he did, the glider's nose dipped, the flapping stopped, and he appeared to be in control again.

"Whew," George said. "He's okay. Boy, that was scary. For a second I thought he was going to cr—" She stopped talking, mouth open.

The glider had once more come to a shuddering stop. This time, though, before the pilot could do anything, it started to fall, spinning toward the ground just in front of them.

"He *is* crashing!" Bess screamed.

Chapter

Two

Wᴇ'ᴅ ʙᴇᴛᴛᴇʀ sᴇᴇ what we can do to help," Nancy said, already running.

Bess didn't move at first but watched in horror as the glider crashed in a crumple of aluminum tubing and gaily colored material.

Seconds later all three of them had reached the crash site. Nancy was afraid they might be too late to help. The pilot wasn't moving, and the fall had jarred his protective helmet loose. As Nancy knelt beside the still form of the pilot, she saw a spill of shiny auburn hair surrounding the pretty face of the now unconscious young woman.

"That's no guy!" Bess said, stating the obvious. "Do you think she's going to be okay, Nancy?"

"There's no blood that I can see," Nancy said over her shoulder to her friend. "But she's out cold." Nancy ran her hands along the girl's arms and legs. "Nothing seems to be broken. Still, I think you should take the jeep and go for help, George."

"Looks like help's on the way." Shielding her eyes from the glare of the sun, George was looking up the road at a dark green minivan that was barreling toward them.

With a spatter of gravel the minivan skidded to a stop. The driver and his passenger were already out and running before the loosened gravel had a chance to settle back into place. Both were dressed in what Nancy decided must be the club's unisex uniform for staffers: khaki shorts and dark green polo shirts.

As the young female passenger dropped to her knees beside the fallen woman, Nancy recognized her as Marva Phillips—there was no mistaking the elfin face and cap of honey blond hair. She'd seen a photo of Marva in the club's brochure. There'd also been a photo of her companion, from whose tanned features and sun-streaked light brown hair Nancy recognized Marva's assistant, Gil Forrest.

"Oh, no!" Marva cried out as she saw the injured woman's face. "It's Lisa Gregson."

Marva seemed to be speaking to no one in particular as she blurted out, "Is she—is she—"

Nancy started to answer. But before she could, Marva had leapt to her feet and was facing the driver of the van. "What kind of lousy instructor are you, Gil?" she yelled. "This is all your fault. How could you have allowed this to happen? Lisa's hurt—maybe dead." Marva nervously put a hand to her mouth. "Oh, this is awful—just awful."

"She's not dead," Nancy said in a voice loud enough to get the club owner's attention. "But she is injured and could have a concussion. A doctor should examine her as soon as possible."

At that moment Lisa's eyes fluttered open. "Wh-what happened?" she asked weakly. Then her eyes focused and she looked past Nancy to Gil. "I don't understand. Something was wrong with the glider. . . . wouldn't respond to . . ." She winced suddenly, obviously in pain. "Ouch, that hurts," she said after touching the side of her head.

"This young lady's right," Marva said, meaning Nancy. "Lisa should see a doctor. Maybe we should take her to the hospital in Newport."

"No!" At the suggestion Lisa had jerked up to a sitting position. "The last thing I want is to go to any hospital." Gil was supporting

11

Lisa, his arm about her shoulders. "I'm all right," Lisa insisted. "I just have a little head-ache. That's all."

"Well, if you're sure . . ." Marva appeared to hesitate. "All right. But we're going to call the club doctor and have him check you over, just to be sure. In the meantime, you've got to take it easy." She turned to Gil. "We'll drive her to the infirmary." She paused, then gave a little shake of her head. "Gil, I'm sorry I snapped at you," she said in a lowered voice. "We'll talk about this later."

Gil's reply was a cold shrug as he helped Lisa to her feet.

Marva turned to speak to Nancy. "Thank you for your help." She put out her hand. "I'm Marva Phillips. I own Club High Adventure." She nodded her head in Gil's direction. "And this is my assistant, Gil Forrest."

Nancy smiled. "I'm Nancy Drew, and these are my friends." She introduced Bess and George, then suggested they ride back to the club together. "It would be a good chance for us to talk," Nancy added.

Marva managed a wan smile. "I'm so glad you're all finally here. And, yes, I think it'd be a good idea for us to ride back together." She glanced at Gil. "Can you handle Lisa by your-self?"

"I can manage," Gil answered curtly.

Nancy couldn't help noticing the unhappy

frown that slipped across Marva's face as Gil held his arm longer than necessary around Lisa's waist.

"Oh, Marva." Lisa smiled at her sweetly, then allowed her head to drop weakly on to Gil's shoulder. "Would you mind stopping by my cabin to let my roommates know I'm all right? I was supposed to meet them for lunch. Now that I'm going to the infirmary, I don't want them to worry."

"Sure, Lisa. I'll be happy to do that." Nancy could see Marva was barely able to keep her eyes off Gil as he helped Lisa into the van and went around to the driver's side. Finally, as Gil drove off with Lisa, Marva turned back to Nancy.

"I can't tell you how glad I am to see you," she said again. "Especially after this accident."

"After all the threats, do you think this really was an accident?" Nancy asked as she stepped over to the damaged glider and began to examine it. But since she didn't know much about hang gliders, she wasn't sure what to look for.

"I hate to think it could have been deliberate," Marva said as she watched Nancy. "But it is possible. Lisa *was* the first to receive a threat."

"But it could have been an accident, couldn't it?" Bess had picked up Lisa's helmet and was handing it to Marva.

"Yes, but Lisa's had some experience. And, despite what I said to Gil, he is one of the best hang-gliding instructors around."

"What Lisa said about the glider not responding makes me wonder," Nancy said thoughtfully as she stood back from the glider. "I think you should send someone out to see that no one touches this glider until Gil can look it over. I'd like his opinion on whether or not the glider was sabotaged."

"I'll do that," Marva agreed as the four walked to the jeep and climbed in. "Let me show you to your cabin. We can talk afterward."

Marva directed as Nancy drove. "Take the road that cuts to the left, past the clubhouse," she said as they drove past the main complex.

Gil had parked the minivan and was helping Lisa from the front passenger seat. A crowd of curious guests had gathered.

"I honestly hope she's as fit as she looks," Marva commented drily. "I know it's insensitive of me, but if anything is seriously wrong with her, my insurance could easily be canceled. And her father is the kind of man who would sue me for everything I have."

"What kind of insurance company would cancel a policy because of one accident?" George asked. "That's what insurance companies are for."

"Not when one accident is coupled with

everything else that's been going on here," Marva said. "Oh, Nancy, you've just got to help me. I'm already at my wit's end. And after this"—she gestured to Lisa hanging onto Gil's arm—"I just don't know what to do."

"That's why I'm here," Nancy assured her. "To do whatever I can to find out who's behind these threats. I won't leave until I do."

Marva smiled a little and relaxed enough to point out a tiny flowered meadow and stream where, she said, deer came to drink every evening. Nancy was only a little surprised that Marva could go so quickly from being proud and confident to being on the verge of tears. The threats were clearly taking their toll on her.

They continued on the road several more yards to an area of individual redwood-and-glass cabins, perched in the middle of dense woods but still within a hundred yards of the rocky coastline. Marva directed Nancy to pull up in front of the third one.

"Every cabin has its own special view," she explained as she helped them with their luggage. "Yours looks out over the mountains. The one next to you"—she pointed to a cabin just visible between the trees—"looks onto that deer-grazing area. That's Lisa's cabin. Her roommates are Sara Lakin and Kirsten Peterson. Oh, that reminds me. I'll have to tell them about Lisa as soon as we're finished."

Marva didn't look too eager to break the news to Lisa's roommates about her accident. But she shook herself and tried to smile as she let Nancy, Bess, and George into their cabin.

Inside, the girls' cabin was a subtle combination of luxury and comfort. Two roomy bedrooms, each with its own full bath, opened onto a living room with a cathedral ceiling and stone fireplace.

"This must be the VIP cabin!" Bess exclaimed, dropping her yellow duffel bag on the cream-colored carpet. She plopped down on one of the two turquoise couches that flanked the fireplace. "All I need now is something to eat. It seems like hours since we had breakfast. And with the time change, it's way past our lunchtime."

With the smile of a proud owner, Marva turned to Bess. "There's a minikitchen behind the entertainment wall." She motioned to a freestanding wood-paneled section of wall that held a large TV, VCR, stereo, and enough video and audio cassettes to keep anyone happy for a year. "There's a refrigerator stocked with soft drinks and fruit, and there are plenty of munchies in the cabinets."

"Super!" Bess jumped up. "Anyone besides me want anything?"

"Something tall and cold sounds good," George said.

"Make that two"—Nancy turned to Marva —"three?" Marva nodded. "Would you mind filling us in before you see Lisa's friends?"

"Not at all," Marva said, perching on the arm of one sofa. "The sooner you know all the details, the sooner you can get started."

While Nancy and George sat down on matching armchairs, Bess went into the kitchen. She was back quickly with a tray of sodas and a plate of crackers and cheese.

"When did these death threats start?" Nancy asked, trying to be as gentle as possible. "And how many have there been?"

Marva thought for a moment. "Actually the first one was right after Lisa and her friends arrived. I think hers was the first. At least she was the first person to come to me about it."

"Tell me," Nancy said, "did any of your guests leave suddenly before then? Without explanation? Or did you notice any one of them acting particularly nervous?"

"I really don't remember." Marva nervously ran a slender hand through her short cropped hair. "But I think that's because so many other things were going wrong. Besides, it's not unusual for a guest to leave at a moment's notice. A lot of them are famous or important and their schedules are always changing."

"You mentioned other things going wrong. Like what?" Nancy asked.

17

"Oh, I don't know," Marva answered with a thoughtful frown. "I guess they're just the usual things that only go wrong when you're short of money." Marva ticked them off on her fingers. "The sauna heater went out. A guest left the water running in his tub so that it ruined the entire carpet in one of the cabins. The door to the walk-in freezer broke so that it can't be opened from the inside. The part is on order, but it's taking forever to get here. One of the kitchen help quit because he was accidentally locked inside for a few minutes." She laughed bitterly. "If it's not one thing, it's another."

Nancy nodded sympathetically. "I can see that."

"Also, my financial situation is not that great," Marva went on. "Which is, as I explained on the phone, why I can't call in the police. If anything leaked to the press about the threats, I'd have a hard time getting new customers, or managing to convince the old ones to come back. That would be the end of Club High Adventure."

"I understand," Nancy said reassuringly. "Now tell me about the threatening letters. You mentioned each was different, but maybe there's a pattern."

"If there is, I can't see it. But I have them in my office if you want to take a look." Marva went on, absently picking up her glass and running a finger down the side, making a mark in the frost. "Lisa's was a note. Just three words, written in regular ballpoint pen. 'You will die.' What's so upsetting is that the note was on my personal club stationery."

"How do you think the writer got to your stationery?" Nancy asked. "Do you keep it where a guest or employee could get to it?"

"No. It's expensive. I keep it in my desk drawer."

"So either a guest ran across it while riffling through your desk," Nancy mused, "or an employee knew about it." She shook her head. "Too early to tell."

"Strange," Marva said thoughtfully. "Until now I hadn't considered whether it was a guest or an employee. I guess I didn't want to think about it too hard."

"What about the second one?" Nancy prompted. Bess and George were also listening attentively at this point.

"Sara got that one. A couple of days later. She came back from the club pool and found an eight-by-ten photo of herself taped to the mirror in her bathroom." Marva drew in her breath sharply as she remembered. "Someone must have taken it without her noticing— there was a heavy, black X scratched through her face."

"Oh, that's awful," Bess exclaimed, putting down a bit of cracker and cheese she'd been about to pop in her mouth.

"How about that other girl—Kirsten?" George jumped in with a question. "Did she get one, too?"

Marva nodded. "The very next day. She goes for a long run every morning before breakfast. When she picked up her Walkman one morning she found a strange cassette in it."

Bess leaned forward, eyes wide. "What was on it?"

"The voice was disguised, muffled so it was impossible to tell if it was a man or woman," Marva said. "But the message was clear enough. 'Keep an eye on your friends, or you might find yourself in serious danger.'"

"Wow!" Bess rolled her eyes.

"Hmmm. I think we've got a creative criminal to deal with." Nancy chewed on her lower lip. "You mentioned there were several threats when we talked on the phone. That's only three."

"Yes. The others were mostly notes that turned up in the guest cabins." Marva paused. "Every time the guest who found one swore they'd locked the cabin before leaving."

Nancy nodded, storing away this bit of information.

"Larry Quinn—he's a businessman from

Portland—got the most recent one last night. I didn't see it, though. He just told me about it."

"Wouldn't he show it to you?" George asked.

"He said he threw it away. He thought it was a stupid prank by someone who gets his kicks trying to frighten people. Like someone who makes obscene phone calls."

"That's one possibility," Nancy said.

"Gil agrees with him." Marva glanced down at the third finger of her left hand where a diamond sparkled. "Gil's my fiancé, you know."

Nancy thought that for someone who was engaged, Marva was smiling a little unhappily. She hadn't known Marva and Gil were engaged, but she'd certainly noticed Lisa flirting with Gil.

"Gil sees the threats as just one more thing that's going wrong. He's trying very hard to convince me to sell the club." Suddenly she balled her fists and said firmly, "But I refuse. I won't give up."

Marva stood up. "I really should get going," she said. "I have to get back to work, and before that I have to stop in to see Sara and Kirsten."

"I think I have enough to go on for now," Nancy said.

"Let me know if you need anything," Marva said. She walked across the living room, then stopped at the door. "And Nancy," she said, "thanks for coming."

"You're welcome," Nancy answered. "Don't worry, Marva. We'll catch this person." Marva gave Nancy a hopeful smile and let herself out.

"I like her," Bess said positively, after Marva left. "And I think whoever it is who's leaving those death threats is one true creep."

"It doesn't necessarily have to be a guy," George said.

"Right," Nancy said absently, obviously lost in thought. Setting down her glass, she stood up, suddenly alert. "I'm going to get right to work after I unpack and take a quick shower."

As Nancy stood under the shower's warm spray, she went over what Marva had told her. One fact stood out in her mind—the threats had been left in locked cabins. That, along with the theft of Marva's personal note paper, made Nancy decide to concentrate on the employees first.

After toweling dry, Nancy slipped into a pair of denim shorts and a striped soccer shirt. Then she laced running shoes on her feet. Standing before the mirror, she gave her shining hair a few quick strokes. The first thing to do, she decided, would be to go to Marva's office and check through the personnel records. Perhaps she would find a clue that would help her narrow the possibilities.

Nancy stepped into the living room. There

she found a note Bess and George had left her, explaining they had gone for a short walk to explore the club.

Nancy had just put the note down when a piercing scream came from the woods outside the cabin. A moment later there was a sharp knock on the front door, which burst open before Nancy could get to it.

Marva stood there, her face pale beneath her tan. "Larry—Larry Quinn—there's been an accident. . . ." Her voice shook. "I—I think he may have been killed."

Chapter

Three

"QUINN? KILLED?" Nancy quickly stepped to Marva's side and put her hands firmly on Marva's shoulders. "Where is he? What makes you think he's dead?"

"Because he's not moving," Marva cried, fighting back tears. "And he's so pale." She looked frantically at Nancy. "He was hardly even breathing when I left him."

"Where is he?" Nancy tried to get Marva to calm down enough to get some answers. "Where did you leave him?"

"On the cliff trail." She pointed out through the living room's sliding glass door. "There's a trail in back of the cabins that leads to the main complex. Larry was right in front of me. He was walking along, and then the next second he seemed to lose his balance. He fell. He—he hit his head." Marva shook her head, as if to rid herself of the terrible sight.

"Marva, listen to me." Nancy shook Marva by the shoulders. "His injury may not be as bad as you think. In any case, we have to get to him." She looked Marva in the eye. "Pull yourself together and show me where he is."

Marva nodded. "You're—you're right." The color had slowly returned to her cheeks. "I'll show you. Come on." Turning, she sped out the door, Nancy at her heels.

The spot where Marva had left Larry Quinn wasn't far—just beyond Lisa's cabin. Nancy didn't know what she'd find when they got there, but she was glad that help had arrived ahead of them.

Two young men in club uniforms were lifting Larry Quinn onto a stretcher. There were some bruises on his face, and a nasty-looking cut over his left eye was still bleeding. But as he was carried along the trail, Nancy saw that Quinn was breathing easily. It looked as if he'd survive. According to one of the young men, a guest had called for help.

After they'd gone, Nancy saw Marva biting at her upper lip, tears welling up in her eyes.

"Oh, Nancy, I feel horrible about this. *I* should have been the one to get help, not some guest. It was my responsibility." A tear spilled over and slid down her cheek. "I don't know what's happening to me. I'm falling apart. Two near-fatal accidents in the space of a couple of hours. It's too much. The death threats are coming true." She covered her face with her hands.

"Marva, I know how worried you must feel." Nancy put a comforting arm around her shoulders. "But you can't break down now. You have to help me."

"Help—you?" Marva lowered her hands to stare blankly at Nancy. "How?"

"I want to know exactly what happened. You said Quinn was right in front of you, and that he seemed to lose his balance. Do you think he might have tripped on something?"

"Ummmm . . ." Marva frowned, obviously trying to remember the details. "No. It was more like his feet suddenly went out from under him. If it had happened a few feet farther on, he might have gone over the cliff. The trail narrows and it's a straight fall of eight hundred feet. But what I don't understand is why Larry Quinn was on this trail alone. It's clearly marked that no one should take it alone—except staff. It is quite dangerous in spots."

Nancy nodded. While Quinn was being carried away, she had noticed the signs warning guests away from the trail.

"It could be as simple as Quinn losing his balance because of his shoe soles," she told Marva. "Or maybe a pebble slid on the ground. Show me where he fell. I'd like to check out the spot for myself."

Marva pulled herself together enough to point Nancy to a piece of the trail ten feet away. Nancy walked slowly in that direction, her eyes fastened to the ground. It was a dirt trail, solidly packed from people walking over it. Nothing looked suspicious until she reached the place where Quinn had lost his balance. There, the dirt appeared to be loose.

Looking around her, Nancy found what she needed—a stout stick. She began to dig. A few seconds later she looked up at Marva. "I think I've found something."

"What is it?" Marva had joined her and was peering at the hole Nancy had dug. "I don't see anything."

"Here. These three round rocks." Nancy poked at the stones she'd uncovered. "They're not very large, but if I'm right, they were big enough to do the job. I'd guess someone deliberately dug them up, then replaced them and added a thin cover of dirt so that anyone stepping on them would slide just enough to lose their balance." And possibly go right over the cliff, she thought.

"You're saying it definitely was not an accident, then?" Marva turned wide eyes toward Nancy. "Someone was deliberately trying to kill Larry?"

"Well, give him a scare at least," Nancy said cautiously.

"What are you going to do now?" Marva put her hand on Nancy's arm. "You've got to hurry and solve this mystery. All those people who've received threats—their lives are in danger, too."

"I'd like to start by taking a look at the actual notes," Nancy said.

"Good idea," Marva agreed, nodding. She seemed to have finally regained her composure. "Let's head over to my office."

Forty minutes later, Nancy and Marva were sitting in Marva's office. Nancy was sitting on a sofa across from Marva's desk, with the notes scattered around her. She held up the defaced photo of what was probably a pretty Kirsten Peterson and looked at it a last time. Then Nancy got up, picked up the evidence, and set it back down on Marva's desk.

"I thought if I saw these"—she waved a hand at the pile of crumpled notes—"I'd find a lead. But they're not telling me any more than you already have."

After seeing the disappointed look on

Marva's face, Nancy added a hopeful note, "But, look, sometimes I'll see something and not actually realize where it fits in until much later. It was still a good idea for me to go through these." She smiled, trying to give Marva some encouragement.

Marva was about to answer when the door opened and Gil Forrest walked in. After acknowledging Nancy's presence with a quick hello, he turned to Marva.

"Thought you'd be glad to know the doctor's given Lisa a clean bill of health," he said impersonally. "Nothing more than some minor bruises. Apparently the ground was soft enough where she landed, and even though her helmet came off on impact, it did protect her head. But he suggested she stay the night in the infirmary to get some rest."

"That's good to hear," Marva replied, clearly scanning Gil's eyes for some sign of emotion. "I'm relieved Lisa wasn't seriously hurt. But how about Larry Quinn? How's he?"

"Larry?" Gil stared at Marva in confusion. "What about him?"

"He had an accident. He was hurt. Badly." Nancy noticed an edge creeping into Marva's voice. "If you were really at the infirmary, like you said you were, you must have seen him. That's where Josh and Ken took him."

"Well, I didn't *just* come from there," Gil

said, frowning at the way Marva was treating him. "What happened?" He looked from Marva to Nancy.

"Actually, *accident* would be the wrong word to use," Marva went on. "He almost went off the trail."

"There were some loose rocks on the trail," Nancy explained. "He lost his balance, slipped, and hit his head on a rock. That's really all we know right now."

"Just how bad is he?"

"I don't really know," Marva admitted. With a shaking hand she picked up the phone. "I'm not even sure if he got to the infirmary safely. What's wrong with me? I should have called." She punched out the infirmary's number.

"If he's up to it, I'd like to talk to him," Nancy told her.

Marva answered with a quick nod.

Nancy tried to overhear the conversation, but Marva kept her voice low. From what she could tell, however, it didn't look good.

"Well, he's going to be all right," Marva said with a sigh after she had hung up. "But Dr. Hill said it is fairly serious. He wants to take Larry to the hospital in Newport for X rays. And he wants him to spend the night—just in case."

Swiveling in her chair, she faced Nancy. "I'm sorry, but Dr. Hill said Larry wasn't in any shape to talk. Not now. Maybe tomorrow."

"I'm sorry, too," Nancy replied. "He might have been able to give me a clue."

"Clue?" Gil lifted his eyebrows. "Come on, Marva. Aren't you letting this get out of hand? I think you're overreacting. Some jerk with a warped sense of humor sends a few guests fake death threats. Then there're a couple of accidents. And you're building it up into some kind of murder plot."

"Gil!" Marva's voice was shrill, her eyes glittering with the beginnings of real anger. "You don't understand—"

"No!" Gil held up a hand, stopping her. "You don't understand, Marva. Club High Adventure is devoted to risky sports. That's what we're all about, remember? We've had accidents before. And we'll probably have them again."

"I know all that, Gil. And I still say I'm not overreacting. These 'accidents' are different." She leaned forward in her desk chair and stared hard at him. "The problem I see is that you're not reacting at all."

"Marva—" Gil tried a soothing smile.

"Stop that, Gil." She pointed a finger at him. "Stop treating me as if I were one of your pretty little students who can't tell the difference between up and down. What's happening here should be as obvious to you as it is to

31

me—and Nancy." She nodded once in Nancy's direction. "Those threats weren't the work of some sick prankster. They're real." She slapped her desktop with the palm of her hand, sending papers scattering. "Real!"

"Marva, calm down, please," Gil pleaded.

"Oh, you can be so dumb at times, Gil." Glaring at him, Marva cried out, "How many accidents have to happen before you realize that this is serious? There's someone here at the club—right here—who's either trying to destroy me by destroying the club's reputation, or is a homicidal maniac. These accidents—whatever you want to call them—are enough to convince me."

"I—I— Oh, I don't know what to say anymore, Marva," Gil said with resignation. "I think the best thing I can do is leave you alone to cool off. When you want to talk quietly about this, let me know." Turning, Gil stormed out of Marva's office.

"Oh no," Marva moaned. Her fury disappeared when Gil left, and she collapsed back against her chair. "Maybe I should just give up. Do what Gil wants me to do. Sell the club. Perhaps if I went away all this would stop and the guests would be safe."

"Marva, I know you can't mean that," Nancy said gently. "This place *is* you. With you gone, Club High Adventure could never be what you've made it. Giving it up won't accomplish anything—you've got to see this through."

Watching her reaction, Nancy saw Marva's inner strength begin to return. Finally Marva took a deep breath and shook off what was left of her panic.

"Thanks for the pep talk, Nancy," she said. "I guess I needed that. I just wish Gil felt the same way. But in time he'll come around, I'm sure." She straightened in her chair. "I'm making you one promise. No matter what happens, no one will force me out. Not even Gil Forrest!"

Chapter

Four

NANCY SAW by the set of Marva's jaw and the fire in her blue eyes that her resolve was genuine. Nancy decided that with Marva once again in control, it was time to get on with her investigation.

"I'd like to take a look inside Larry Quinn's cabin," she told Marva. "I may be able to find the note he said he threw away."

"Of course," Marva answered. "I'm sure he'd understand. You'll find his cabin on the other side of yours from where Sara and Kirsten's is."

Turning away from her desk, Marva walked

over and opened a wall cabinet. Rows of loose keys hung on individual hooks, with cabin numbers printed above each one. Marva reached in and took a key from the number 8 hook. She frowned slightly. "Strange. There should be two spare keys here, and there's only one."

The small detail didn't escape Nancy's eyes. "Who else might have taken one?" she asked.

"I can't think of anyone." Marva shrugged. "Well, maybe Larry lost his, and Gil gave him the other spare. But normally when that happens, Gil lets me know."

"Um-hmm." Nancy nodded. "But what if our local joker decided he needed to take a look in that cabin as well?" Reaching down, she picked up and pocketed the key Marva had placed on the desk. "If so, I hope he didn't find what he was looking for."

Nancy said goodbye to Marva, who returned determinedly to work. In the hall just outside the office, Nancy found Gil. He was staring moodily out of a window. Nancy paused to talk to him.

"Sorry to disturb your thoughts." Gil jumped at the sound of her voice. "Did you get a chance to check out that damaged glider?" she asked when she had his attention.

"Not yet." He gave her an annoyed scowl.

"If you recall, I had a few things to do, like taking care of Lisa's injuries." Then he hesitated. "I, uh, had some other things to take care of," Gil explained limply. "But don't worry. I'll get to it soon."

"Good." Nancy looked at him evenly. "The sooner, the better," she told him before walking away toward the main door.

Leaving the complex, Nancy headed for the cabin area along the cliff trail. Although the loose rocks had probably been removed by the groundskeeper, she knew that walking the path would give her a better picture of the event.

As she walked, Nancy thought the trail didn't even seem to be that dangerous. It was quite wide where it traced the cliff edge, and there was a retaining wall. The worst the trail could do was scare someone who was afraid of heights.

When Nancy reached the final bend before turning off for Quinn's cabin, she found her way blocked by a large, burly man. He appeared to be in his midfifties, and was obviously in excellent physical condition. He was nearly a head taller than Nancy's five feet, seven inches, and at least a hundred pounds heavier. And all of it muscle, Nancy thought, lifting her face to stare into eyes that glowered back at her.

"Excuse me," she said, attempting to pass.

"What are you doing on this trail?" the man demanded. "Didn't you see the red marker on the tree at the trail head? Guests aren't supposed to use this trail alone. It's too dangerous."

"Sorry, I didn't realize," Nancy said. No use broadcasting who she was. People would find out in their own time.

She noticed the man had on the dark green shirt of a staffer. "Next time I'll make sure I'm not alone," Nancy said placatingly.

Hearing her apology, the man lost his forbidding look. A smile crossed his face. "Just don't want to see any of the guests get hurt unnecessarily." He put out his hand. "My name's Al Hunt, by the way. I'm the rock-climbing instructor. Call me Uncle Al. Everyone else does."

"Okay." She shook his tanned and callused hand. "I'm Nancy Drew. You can call me Nancy."

"Nice to meet you, Nancy." He smoothed his short, graying hair. "I'm sorry for the gruff way I came across just now. Accidents like today's tend to make us a little extra cautious."

"I understand." Nancy smiled back at him.

"Well, I've got to get going. Glad to have you with us." As he started past her, he added,

"Come to one of my classes. You look like the type to enjoy rock climbing."

"Thanks. I'll try to make time," she called after him.

Passing behind Lisa Gregson's cabin a moment later, her thoughts turned to the pretty teenager who had so narrowly escaped serious injury. She wanted to question the girl, but the doctor had ordered her to stay in the infirmary, so Nancy would have to wait until morning. Still, there were Lisa's friends, Sara and Kirsten.

Nancy made a quick decision to put off checking out Quinn's cabin and turned onto the path that led to the front of Sara and Kirsten's cabin.

Nancy's knock was answered by a girl with shiny black hair, cut in a short feathered style that emphasized her deep-set, jade green eyes. Tinted contacts, Nancy observed.

"I'm looking for Sara or Kirsten," she explained after introducing herself.

"Kirsten's not here. I'm Sara." The girl didn't invite Nancy to come in. "I'm just on my way over to the pool to meet someone." She glanced at a slim gold watch on one wrist. "Could you come back later? I really don't want to be late."

A guy, Nancy was willing to bet. With her high-heeled purple sandals, matching lavender string bikini and robe, Sara looked more like she was on her way to meet a date than taking a dip in the pool.

"This won't take long," Nancy promised. "Only a couple of questions. I'm trying to find out more about Lisa's accident. Could you tell me about the threat she got?" Nancy hoped this would stir Sara into asking her inside, but Sara stood her ground.

"Look, I said later, okay?" A slight frown marred Sara's otherwise pretty face. She tapped a polished red nail impatiently against the doorjamb. "I don't have anything to say to you. Nothing that could help. Why don't you wait until you can talk to Lisa? Ask her about it."

Sara pulled the cabin door shut and started to walk past Nancy.

Nancy decided to try another tactic. "Sara," she said, reaching out for the girl as she tried to pass her. "I'm only trying to help. You may think you don't have anything to say that would help me figure out what was really behind the accident, but you might be surprised. If we could just go inside, sit down for a few minutes—"

"Look. You don't know Lisa Gregson. I do." Sara yanked her arm free. "That crash was no accident." She started down the cabin's stairs, leaving Nancy standing there.

Nancy watched the girl as she took the steps

awkwardly and stumbled along the redwood-chip path in her high heels.

Sara Lakin is completely out of her element here at Club High Adventure, Nancy thought as she made her way in the opposite direction toward Quinn's cabin. I bet she'd prefer being at a luxury resort having her nails wrapped and going to parties. So what is she really doing here? Nancy stored the question away with the other pieces of the puzzle she'd collected so far.

Using the key Marva had given her, Nancy let herself into Quinn's cabin. It was similar to hers, except here the color scheme was earth tones, browns and dark greens accented with cream-colored couches and chairs. The living room was neat. A half-filled coffee cup on the counter of the tiny kitchen was the only clutter.

The bedroom was also tidy, except for the unmade bed. A gray suitcase sat squarely on the luggage rack. Through the open door of the bathroom, Nancy could see an organized array of toiletries.

There was nothing there to show that Larry Quinn's behavior in the past few hours had been anything but that of a normal guest. And to Nancy's practiced eye, it was fairly certain that no one else had searched the cabin before she'd arrived.

Especially since this is still here, she thought excitedly, bending to retrieve a wadded piece of paper from the wastebasket beside the dresser.

After smoothing the crumpled sheet of yellow lined paper, she read the message. It was in block letters, written with blue ballpoint pen. "Leave the club today and you'll live. Stay and you'll die."

Whoever was behind this wasn't beating around the bush, Nancy thought as she folded the paper, stuffed it into a pocket of her shorts, and returned to the living room.

Taking one last look around, she pushed open the sliding glass door to the sun deck and stepped out.

Unlike the cabin she shared with Bess and George, this one backed up to a rocky cliff. The far end of the sun deck was supported by long wooden stilts buried into the cliff face. Nancy relaxed for a moment. Taking a deep breath of the tangy salt air, Nancy walked to the railing and leaned against it, letting the sun warm her head.

Far below, sea lions basked on the offshore rocks. Overhead, sea gulls swooped and called to one another in a chorus of noisy screeches.

Closing her eyes, Nancy tilted her face up, warming it in the sun. Club High Adventure could be a very appealing vacation spot, she thought.

As Nancy was basking in the sun, something hit her, hard, against her back.

Nancy's eyes flew open. She felt herself being lifted up and over the side of the deck! She was falling, spread-eagle, with nothing between her and the sharp rocks forty feet below!

Chapter
Five

TUCKING HER KNEES into her chest, Nancy did a tight roll and threw her arms straight up over her head. Clawing with her right hand, she reached out and closed her fingers around one of the upright bars supporting the railing. She tried not to look down at the waves crashing below her.

Tears sprang to her eyes as her shoulder was wrenched from the bone-jarring stop she'd made. But she hung on and swung like a pendulum from her right hand.

She was safe for the moment. She tried to catch her breath, but how long could she hold on before her fingers and shoulder gave out?

Even worse, wouldn't the person who had to have shoved her try to finish her off?

Nancy listened for footsteps on the deck above, but none sounded. Nancy's shoulder was hot with pain.

She thought for an instant about calling for help, but knew that any cries of hers would be lost in the screeching of the gulls. Their noise must have prevented her from hearing her attacker approach.

She was hanging facing away from the house. Quickly, before she could consider the additional pain, she threw her body to the left and grabbed another upright support with her left hand.

It was now a simple matter of inching up, hand over hand, until she reached the top rail.

Nancy used all of her strength to pull her body upward with her left arm until she could grab for the next higher bar. Before she could lose her momentum, Nancy grabbed for the top and last bar with her right hand.

With a final heave, Nancy shimmied up and over the railing and finally collapsed onto the deck. Except for the throbbing in her shoulder, she knew she was okay.

Nancy's instincts told her that the time it had taken to pull herself back up had also given her attacker the chance he, or she, needed to escape. Still, Nancy searched the cabin—just in case. Picking up the poker from the fireplace for protection, she crept through the rooms, looking behind every door and in the shower. The cabin was empty.

More determined than ever to get to the bottom of the mystery, Nancy hurried back to her own cabin. Her "accident" had left her aching and disheveled. She wanted to clean up and change into fresh clothes.

Bess and George were there to greet her. Bess had been to the pool and was now wrapped in a yellow terry robe, toweling her hair dry.

Looking up and seeing Nancy come through the door, she stopped drying her hair and rushed to her. "Nancy," she cried. "What happened? You're a wreck."

"I'll second that," George added from the doorway of their shared bedroom. "Looks like you were on the wrong end of an argument."

"Yeah, I never got a word in," Nancy joked grimly. Flopping down on one of the couches, she told them what had happened. "Of course I didn't get a look at who pushed me," she finished.

George shuddered. "I could have been walking right by there when it was happening. I got back from a hike along the trails only a few minutes ago."

"Did you see anyone on the path in front of Quinn's cabin? Anyone at all?" Nancy asked.

"Nope. Only a couple so wrapped up in each

other that they practically bumped into me before I could get out of their way." George shook her head. "No one else."

"Probably whoever it was slipped through the trees, instead of using the path. Someone who knows his way around very well."

"Does that mean you've already got some idea who's behind all this?" Bess asked expectantly.

"Just the start of a theory," Nancy replied. "But it's a long way from being complete. Right now, we don't really know anything definite about what happened to Lisa Gregson or Larry Quinn."

"What's the plan?" George asked. "What do you want us to do?"

"Nothing right now, George. What I have to do next, I have to do alone."

"Well, if you're not going to let us in on your plan, at least be careful," Bess admonished.

"Yes, Nan, watch yourself," George echoed her cousin's concern. "Whoever is making the threats must know you're here to investigate. He already tried to kill you once, and he's sure to try again."

"I know," Nancy said, her blue eyes serious. "And, believe me, I don't intend to be such an easy target again."

Because it was getting late, Nancy changed her mind about showering and putting on fresh clothes. She took only enough time to go into the bathroom and wash her hands and face.

A few minutes later, after knocking to make sure no one was in Lisa, Kirsten, and Sara's cabin, she deftly picked the lock on their door, and slipped inside.

Remembering Sara's outburst that "the accident was no accident," Nancy wanted to find out more about the girl.

It wasn't difficult figuring out which bedroom belonged to Lisa Gregson. A gold necklace with her first name etched on its pendant was tossed on the dresser. Stuck into the edge of the dresser mirror was a color snapshot of Lisa and a good-looking boy, who would have looked even better if he hadn't been scowling into the camera lens.

Nancy pulled open each of the three drawers in the dresser and found only piles of expensive clothes jammed in every which way. Apparently, Lisa came from a wealthy family and had absolutely no respect for the designer fashions she was able to afford.

Finally, in a drawer of the bedside table Nancy hit pay dirt. She found a half-finished letter, dated the night before. Nancy scanned it.

My adorable Roy,
  I can't tell you how much I miss you. I have your picture where I can look at it

constantly. I wish I could reach out and touch you as easily as I touch the photo. I hate my father for making me stop seeing you. He just doesn't understand how it is with us. He never will. I just know it. But I have a plan that is going to make him sorry—really sorry.

The letter ended there. Nancy replaced it carefully. Searching further, she discovered a clipping and a picture from a newspaper. She picked it up to look at it closely.

The photo was blurred, but Nancy was fairly certain the girl in it was Lisa. She was hand-cuffed to a police officer, as was a boy. Even though he had his free hand over his face, Nancy recognized the boy from the other photo. He and Lisa were about to step into a police cruiser.

The caption under the photo read, "Lisa Gregson, daughter of prominent real estate businessman Greg Gregson, was arrested for shoplifting today. This is the second time in three months for Miss Gregson."

It looked like Lisa didn't lead a typical teenage life, Nancy thought, tapping a finger against the worn edge of the clipping. Could she be the one behind the threats? What did she mean about making her father sorry? Could the letter to her boyfriend mean that the accident that day—

A noise interrupted her thoughts. It was the faint sound of a key being turned in the front door. Either Sara or Kirsten had come back to the cabin. Nancy was about to be caught breaking and entering.

Trying not to make any noise, Nancy placed the clipping back into the drawer, then slid it shut. She glanced around, looking for a way out.

The window—but it was too high and too small.

Nancy looked desperately for another escape route. She was about to slip out of Lisa's room when she heard the front door open. Footsteps crossed the entry and were heading her way.

Nancy was trapped.

Chapter

Six

So what did you do?" Bess asked, eagerly leaning forward across the dining table. She kept her voice low so the other guests wouldn't hear.

"Yes, how did you escape without being found out?" George added quietly.

Nancy stopped buttering a roll to answer. "I'd figured out Lisa didn't share a bedroom. So it was pretty good odds that whoever was in the living room wouldn't come into Lisa's room. So I just hid in the closet, and when I heard the other bedroom door close I sneaked out and left the cabin by the front door."

"You've got guts." Bess speared a cherry tomato, dipped it in dressing, and popped it into her mouth. "It's a good thing you're the detective, and not me. I would've panicked and tried to think up some unbelievable story for her roommate. Guess I don't have the stomach to be an investigator."

"No, your stomach is too busy consuming food," George teased her cousin.

"And is this food good," Bess answered, not at all bothered by George's remark. "As far as I'm concerned, Nan, we can take forever to solve this case. When I'm not working, I'll lie around the pool and eat."

"And get fat," George added under her breath. "Maybe you should consider doing a little jogging."

"Uh-uh." Bess shook her head. "You know jogging's not my thing. But maybe a little after-dinner dancing might be beneficial." She smiled at the retreating figure of a six-foot-tall hunk who had just passed their table.

"Back to the case," George said in a low tone, looking around to make sure there was no possibility of being overheard. "Do you really think it could be Lisa Gregson who's behind all this?"

"I'll say this much." Nancy took a sip of her ice water. "I consider her a definite suspect. She's a girl who's apparently desperate for

51

attention. And desperate people do desperate things."

"But hold on," George argued. "Unless she had an accomplice, how could she have been in Quinn's cabin, pushing you over the railing, and be in the infirmary at the same time?"

"That occurred to me," Nancy replied. "I called the infirmary before dinner. No one was there, except Lisa, during that time. Even the nurse had stepped out for a little while. So Lisa doesn't have an alibi. She could easily have left, gone to Quinn's cabin, and returned without being seen. Especially if she went through the woods."

"But what about Lisa's accident?" Bess asked. "I can't believe anyone would stage an accident like that on purpose. She could have been killed."

"We still don't know if the glider was tampered with," Nancy said with a shrug. "Lisa has had some experience with hang gliding. So it's possible she could fake a problem that only *looked* dangerous." Nancy reached for the salt.

"Anyway," she went on, "I'll know more tomorrow. On my way over here tonight, I stopped and signed up for a hang-gliding lesson early in the morning. I'll talk to Gil Forrest about the damaged glider then, too. He should have had time to check it out."

"I should take the class with you," George suggested. "I could keep my eye on Gil."

"I've already signed you up," Nancy answered her friend with a grin.

"Well, that's fine for you guys. But I'm going to stay on the ground where it's safe," Bess said. "Now, for tonight, I want to stop thinking about the case and start dancing."

Bess shoved her chair back and stood up. "I think I see my partner now," she said mischievously.

Early the next morning Nancy and George were standing, along with five other students, at the top of a gentle slope at the far end of a meadow. Gil Forrest was talking to them, a row of gliders behind them. Their multicolored sails were bright against the green grass.

The students all wore standard orange jumpsuits. Nancy cradled her helmet in her arms as she listened to Gil introduce them to the sport of hang gliding.

"First, let me assure you that there is nothing complicated about this sport. There are successful twelve-year-old hang-glider pilots. And good gliders don't have to have a lot of strength." Gil glanced in the direction of one of the more petite students.

"But the wings," the petite student spoke up. "They're so huge. How are we supposed to carry those things?"

Gil grinned at her. "The ground maneuvering of what is essentially a large kite—with about a twenty-two-foot wing span for women, and a twenty-six-foot span for guys—can be a bit of *fun* to get used to at first." There were a couple of groans. "But, I promise"—Gil held up a hand—"it's easier than you'd believe. And once you're in the air, you'll be very glad you have all that sail to play with."

"You just said the magic word," a good-looking blond guy yelled out. "When do we get to do that? Go into the air? I thought you had to jump off a cliff, or something. But I don't see one around here."

"Whoa!" Gil smiled. "We're not going to do any jumping off cliffs for a while. You'll need a few lessons under your belt before you tackle that sort of thing."

"Then what do we do?" the blond guy yelled back with a grin. "Just run and jump into the air and hope we take off?"

"You've got it," Gil told him and grinned back. "And since you're so smart, I'm going to let you go first. Come up here with me and we'll get this harness on you."

There was some easy laughter as the boy swaggered boldly up to Gil. "What's your name?" Gil asked.

"Drake Reynolds."

"All right. And thanks for volunteering, Drake." There was another ripple of laughter before Gil went on. "Now, remember, there's nothing difficult about this sport. There aren't many rules. But you want to avoid breaking any of them—"

"Because then you'll crash," a student at the edge of the group interrupted. "Just like Lisa Gregson did, right?"

"We don't know what happened with Lisa," Gil replied in a subdued tone. Nancy noticed a muscle twitch at the corner of the instructor's mouth. Then he recovered smoothly. "But you're right," Gil said. "Ignore the rules, and you *will* find yourself in trouble."

Gil began helping Drake into a harness made of the nylon webbing Nancy recognized as being similar to those used by parachute jumpers.

"One of the first rules," Gil was saying, "is to make sure your equipment—both your harness and glider—are in good condition."

Nancy watched and wondered if Lisa had thought about this before she'd taken off on her last flight.

"Now let's talk about getting off the ground," Gil said. "What makes the glider sail like it does is the wind. When the air flows over the top of the wing surface, the sail creates a vacuum. The air flowing under the wing pushes the glider up as it tries to fill that vacuum."

"That's interesting," George said to Nancy. "I'm going to remember that when we fly back home."

"And the glider is constructed," Gil continued, "so that you can get into the air with minimal wind speed. You're going to be doing just what the Wright brothers did when they first began playing with the idea of flight.

"After you've put on your harnesses and attached yourself to your gliders, you're going to run down this slope and allow the wind to pull you up into the air. You won't be that far off the ground this first time, but it'll seem high enough for most of you." He patted Drake's shoulder. "Even for you, I bet."

"I'm ready." Drake raised a fist into the air. "Let's go for it!"

"All right. Let's go over and hook you up." Gil led Drake and the others to the waiting gliders.

When they had regrouped, Gil went on. "Now to learn how to stay up when you want to stay up. It has to do with the way you maneuver your glider." He put his hand on a large triangle of aluminum tubing fixed to the bottom of the glider. "This is your control bar. Push it forward and the nose lifts, pull it back and the tail lifts, shoving the nose down—"

"Why would you want to push the nose down?" someone asked. "I thought you wanted to stay up."

"Give me a second more and I'll explain why," Gil said. "Remember that wind that is keeping you aloft? Well, if you tilt your nose up too far your glider will stall. In order to get that airflow back, you'll have to tilt your glider's nose down." He paused. "Ignore that rule, and you'll drop like a rock."

"Oh, boy," the small girl spoke. "That does it for me. I've decided to skip this sport." She sat down cross-legged on the grass. "You guys go on without me. I'm sticking to commercial jets."

"That's all right, Vicki," Gil said. "This sport's not for everyone. Anyone else who wants to drop out, please do. Don't feel as if you have to prove something by staying in." He waited, but no one else said anything.

"Okay, we're almost finished." Gil nodded. "You land by using the stall. But you do it only when you get close to the ground. You don't want to crash, you want to land. Simply glide down to the ground, pull your nose up at the proper moment, and there you are—back on good old solid earth."

At the end of her first hour of practice, Nancy discovered she had a real knack for hang gliding. It had taken her only a couple of false starts before she managed to maintain a short but successful flight. She was even able to make simple right and left turns by shifting her body as it hung in a free position in the harness.

"I really love this sport," she told Gil as she slid out of her jumpsuit. "I guess it's about as close as you can get to feeling like a bird."

"Yes—free." Gil agreed with her, and Nancy felt she was in touch with the real Gil—the man Marva loved. "I love it, too." He took the jumpsuit and helmet from her. "You really should keep taking lessons after you go back home. Maybe join a club."

"I think I'll do that—"

"Hey, Nan." George had hurried up and was interrupting. "I don't mean to rush you, but if we're going to make that rock-climbing class at Devil's Rock, we'd better get a move on."

"Okay," Nancy said, lacing up her last hiking boot. "We'd better go." She looked up at Gil. "I wanted to talk to you about the damaged glider. Did you have a chance to go over it?"

"I did. But what I found has me a little puzzled. I can show you now, if you want. Then I can drop you off at Devil's Rock."

The three of them piled into the club van and soon pulled up in front of a utilitarian-looking building behind the main complex.

"So this is all that was wrong?" Nancy asked, running her hand over the small bend in the frame of Lisa's glider. "I would have expected more."

"The thick grass absorbed most of the shock of the landing. There's only that slight damage in the tubing of the leading edge—where you're feeling now." He shook his head. "What disturbs me is that there shouldn't be any bends there at all. The glider came down on its keel, the other end."

"You think this was done deliberately?" Nancy asked, pointing to the broken spot.

"Well, I can't say for sure." He ran a thumb thoughtfully down the side of his face. "But it's possible. And whoever did it knew what he, or she, was doing. Because there's just enough damage to affect the control but not enough that an experienced pilot would have too much difficulty saving himself." He paused. "Or herself. Remember, Lisa Gregson's logged a lot of time hang gliding."

"Right." Nancy nodded thoughtfully. Then, shaking her head, she said, "I guess we'd better get going."

Back in the van, Gil headed for the foot of the mountains. "That's Devil's Rock," he said, taking one hand off the wheel to point. "Over there."

"I can see how it got its name," George said, peering through the windshield.

Half a mile ahead of them a four-hundred-foot-high dome-shaped rock loomed bare against the dense forest of the mountains behind it. Natural ledges on the otherwise sheer granite front formed an evil-looking devil mask.

"It looks like a dangerous climb," Nancy commented.

"Well, it can be. But any serious climb has its dangers."

"It doesn't scare me," George said bravely.

"Here we are." Gil slowed the van to a stop. "This is as close as we can get by road. That trail over there will take you up the side to the top. Normally the class meets down here, then goes up together. You're a few minutes late, so they've probably gone on ahead."

"We're both in good shape," Nancy said as she pushed down on the door handle. "I don't think it'll take us long to catch up."

"Hope you enjoy the class." Gil leaned over to pull the door shut after they got out. "Uncle Al is a good instructor. He'll teach you everything there is about rock climbing."

With a wave at the departing van, Nancy and George turned and started up the trail. The climb was steep and after several minutes the two had to pause to catch their breath.

"So, what do you think?" George asked, leaning back against a warm rock. "Do you think Lisa could have sabotaged her own glider?"

"It looks bad for her, doesn't it?" Nancy remarked, bending down to tighten the laces on her hiking boots. "But the glider could have gotten that small dent another way, too. Maybe when it was loaded into the van, or taken out. Lisa could have forgotten her preflight check." She straightened up. "It was pretty tough to spot. Gil had to show me where it was."

"I don't know," George argued. "I say Lisa did it herself, to get attention."

"But we need some hard evidence before we decide," Nancy replied. She reached over to pat George on the arm. "If you've got your breath, let's go. We have another lesson before the day's over."

George laughed and took the lead. "Right, boss," she said.

After ten minutes of rough climbing, Nancy and George reached the top. When they got there, they found a class of eight students grouped about Uncle Al, the bear of a man Nancy remembered from the day before.

They were standing on the top of Devil's Rock in the middle of an open area, about the size of a basketball court. All around them was a panorama of ocean, mountains, and forest.

Uncle Al was demonstrating the various types of knots used by rock climbers. As Nancy and George quietly took their places at the back of the group, Nancy noticed the instructor didn't have everyone's attention. A couple of guys were punching each other good-naturedly, obviously enjoying some private joke.

"They'd better cut that out," George whispered to Nancy. "If Uncle Al were glaring at me the way he is at those two, I'd be shaking in my boots."

"I don't blame him," Nancy muttered. "This isn't exactly the safest place in the world to horse around."

Uncle Al had stopped his demonstration in midsentence.

Flinging away the rope he'd been using, he stared openly at the two guys. Then without warning he lunged at them, startling Nancy and the others.

Still moving, Uncle Al reached out a muscular arm and grabbed at the nearer, and smaller, of the two. The short guy nimbly stepped aside, and Uncle Al's elbow caught the bigger boy in the shoulder. Al's blow sent him way off balance.

A girl screamed, and Nancy and George watched, horrified, as the beefy teenager lost his footing, teetered, and flapped his arms. Almost in slow motion, the boy started to fall backward over the edge of Devil's Rock!

Chapter
Seven

PUMPING HIS MUSCULAR ARMS, the boy managed to throw his weight forward and land sprawled on his stomach across the hard rock surface. He was breathing in ragged gasps, and Nancy saw the color had drained from his face, leaving it a pasty gray.

From the student, Nancy looked to where Al Hunt stood, also breathing hard. He kept staring at the boy until he was sure he was all right. Was that a look of fear Nancy saw in Al's eyes? He must have realized that he had overreacted and that his mistake could have been fatal.

With a shake of his bearlike shoulders, Uncle Al pulled himself together. Walking over to where the student was sitting, the instructor held out his hand.

"Sorry, son," he apologized in a controlled voice, as he helped the boy get up. "Didn't mean to be quite so physical there." He paused. "But it looked like you two were headed for danger. The top of this rock is slippery and it's no place for anyone to act like a six-year-old."

The young man was on his feet now, looking both embarrassed and angry. "We weren't doing anything wrong," he mumbled.

"Well," Uncle Al answered, "I don't take kindly to students who don't pay attention when I'm trying to teach them something that might just save their lives." He had turned his attention from the boy and was talking to the entire group.

"Okay, okay." Nancy saw the student's face had gone from white to red and his eyes were narrowing in anger. He looked as if he was more than ready to lose his temper over being made an example for the rest of the class. "I get the message. You want our undivided attention. You got it, *Uncle* Al."

"Cool it, Ron," his friend advised, seeing how upset he was. He put a hand on the young man's arm. "The guy's just doing his job. Why don't we just sit down and let him do it."

Al had picked up the demonstration rope and was explaining the fundamentals of rappelling. The two young men sat down on a rock outcropping near where Nancy and George were standing.

Despite Al's warning, Nancy found herself listening to their whispered conversation rather than paying attention to the demonstration.

"I don't think that old guy's playing with a full deck," Ron growled. "That was a really crazy thing he pulled on us. He could just as easily have pushed me over as kept me from falling."

"Drop it, will you." His friend was starting to sound annoyed. "It's over. Your problem is that it's just beginning to dawn on you what a jerk you made of yourself in front of everyone."

Ron folded his large forearms across his chest. "Not everyone," he said.

"You bet," his friend answered. "Especially Vicki Kirk. Look—forget it, and she'll forget it. Keep it up, and she'll really know you're a jerk. Take it from me."

"Well . . ." Ron hesitated. "Okay, maybe you're right." Nancy was relieved when the two finally fell silent and turned their attention back to Al, who was beginning to notice their chatter again.

Still, Nancy could hardly wait for the lesson

to be over so she could talk to George about Al's tantrum. It seemed out of character to her.

After an hour of practice in the basic rock-climbing techniques, the class started back down the trail. Nancy and George hung back to bring up the rear. With no one to overhear them, Nancy voiced her concern about Al's strange behavior.

"That really was crazy, the way he acted with those two guys," Nancy said.

"Maybe he's just nervous and jumpy because of what's been happening lately," George suggested.

"Or maybe there's some other reason," Nancy said, frowning.

"Are you adding him to your suspect list?" George asked.

Nancy slowed down to negotiate a steep part of the trail. "I don't think there's any connection between him and Lisa Gregson," she said, holding on to a thin pine tree for support.

"I don't see one either," George admitted.

They had reached a plateau where both girls stopped to take in the view. Nancy's mind turned back to the case.

"But we don't know for sure yet," she said.

"What's the next move?" George asked as they continued down the trail.

"A soda," Nancy laughed. "After all these lessons, I'm thirsty."

"Sounds good to me," George answered. "And I'll bet we find Bess waiting for us."

The two girls made their way back to the main complex and out onto the club's terrace café. Sure enough, Bess was there.

"You never quit, do you?" George asked as she sat down. Just before Nancy and George arrived, Bess had been saying a cheerful goodbye to yet another six feet two of tanned muscle.

"Actually," Bess said, pouting, "I was working on the case. Jed—that's his name—was telling me that Gil and Marva have been having problems for a long time now."

"What kind of problems?" Nancy asked, after she gave the waitress her order. "I know they've been under a lot of pressure lately, what with everything that's been going on at the club."

"Yeah, Bess," George added. "I'll bet that's what Jed, or whatever his name is, meant."

"No, it wasn't," Bess insisted. "I know because I asked him how long it'd been going on. He's known Gil for a while. He said Gil and Marva have always had problems. We even laughed and talked about how for some people that's what a relationship is all about." Bess smiled, obviously going over the conversation again in her head.

George and Nancy exchanged a look. Nancy

didn't think Bess's news was all that significant or important to the case. Except, she thought, that it might give Gil a motive.

Nancy got up. "Sorry, guys, but I have to get going."

"What's up?" George asked.

"I want to go over the employee files before lunch," Nancy said. "I have a feeling I'll find something in there that'll give us a few more pieces to the puzzle."

"You sure you don't want us to come along?" Bess asked halfheartedly.

"No, Bess," Nancy laughed. "You keep asking Jed those questions. Let me know if you find out anything else."

George chuckled. "Since you don't need us, I think I'll take a swim. It's getting hot."

Nancy and George left Bess in the café, and strolled over behind the back of the main complex to where the swimming pools were. They split up, George heading over to the Olympic-size pool, Nancy walking down a short path to the complex's back entrance.

Opening a screen door, Nancy found she was in a long hall, off of which several doors opened into what must have been offices and storage areas.

She had gone no more than a few steps when she heard the sound of angry voices drifting out of one of the rooms. She was sure it was

Gil and Marva, and it sounded as if they were having some sort of lovers' quarrel.

Nancy thought she should turn around and leave quietly so they wouldn't think she'd been eavesdropping, but something about the desperate tone of Marva's voice made her stay in the hall. As their voices grew louder, Nancy inched closer to where they were coming from.

"No, Gil, I won't do it. I won't, I tell you—never." The pitch of Marva's voice rose higher and higher until she sounded hysterical. "Not for you, *not for anyone!*"

"You've got no choice, Marva," Gil answered in cold fury. "You should do what I'm telling you to. Sell the club. Sell it, or I'll—"

"Do what?" Marva screamed back.

For a long moment the only sound that reached Nancy's ears was that of ragged breathing from the other side of the partially open door.

Then Nancy heard Gil and Marva scuffling, followed by a barely stifled sob from Marva.

Nancy was about to burst in on them when she heard Gil's voice raised in anger.

"I won't take much more of this, Marva," Gil cried out.

Marva's only response was another racking sob.

"Sometimes I could just kill you!" Gil shouted.

Chapter

Eight

NANCY STARTED to rush inside when Gil came storming out, almost knocking Nancy down. After giving her an icy look, Gil marched off.

"Marva?" Nancy turned from Gil to peek into the room. "Are you okay?" she asked.

Marva glanced around, startled. "Oh, Nancy." She began to cry all over again.

"I'm sorry, Marva," Nancy said, trying to console her. "I'm sure he didn't mean it."

Marva wiped the tears from her cheeks, then seemed to pull herself together. "You heard?"

Nancy explained that she was on her way to

70

find her when she overheard their fight. "I almost left but stayed because I got worried."

"It's okay." Marva sighed. "I'm sorry you had to hear the stupid way we were both acting." She made a disgusted face, then she looked over Nancy's head, unable to meet her eyes. "We're both under a lot of strain," she said hesitantly.

"I know you are," Nancy answered kindly.

"Gil really has my best interests at heart," Marva said, trying to smooth over the fight. "He's so worried about me that he ends up yelling." She gave Nancy an unhappy little smile. "Gil loves me, and I love him. That's really the bottom line," she said as they walked from the room into the hall.

Marva stopped and turned to Nancy. "You were looking for me?" she asked. "For a minute there, I was so wrapped up in my own problems that I wasn't thinking. Did you need something?"

"Actually I was on my way to your office. I was planning to spend a little time going over your employee records." She glanced down the hall toward the kitchen, where the staff was busy getting ready to serve the noon meal. "But I didn't realize how late it was getting. I suppose it can wait until after lunch."

"I'll be in my office," Marva said. "And thanks for looking out for me," she added. "I can't tell you how much I appreciate what you're doing."

"All in a day's work," Nancy joked as she and Marva parted.

Before returning to her cabin Nancy made a quick detour to the infirmary. She wanted to check on Lisa, but she learned from the nurse that Lisa had been dismissed a couple of hours earlier. Nancy used the phone there to place a call to the hospital to find out about Larry Quinn's condition. It was worse than she had expected—during the night Quinn had slipped into a coma.

Back at her cabin, Nancy worried about how serious the case had gotten. Quinn in a coma, Marva and Gil fighting, and still no clues about who could be responsible for terrorizing Club High Adventure. Without a lead, Nancy couldn't prevent worse things from happening.

While she was changing into white cotton slacks and a red knit shirt, Nancy heard Bess and George return. She went out into the living room to greet them. Maybe if she talked out the case with them, they'd see something she'd missed.

George ran past Nancy into the bedroom. "I'll just be a minute," she said to Nancy. "Can you wait for me to change?" Nancy nodded. Bess, looking fresh and pretty, poked her head into the living room. "You want a soda?" she asked.

"Sounds good," Nancy answered distractedly, curling up on one of the couches.

"Well, now I know everything there is to know about kayaking," Bess announced as she handed Nancy her drink. She plopped back on the other couch. "Jed told me all about it, and I positively love it. It's a super sport."

George stepped out into the living room, wearing red running shorts and a striped yellow-and-blue rugby shirt. "What's up, Nan?" she asked. "You look preoccupied."

"I was thinking about the case," Nancy answered. "There's so much that doesn't add up."

"Like that business up on Devil's Rock, you mean?" George asked.

"How about filling me in?" Bess said. "What about Devil's Rock, wherever that is?"

Nancy realized she hadn't told Bess earlier about their morning's activities. She went over what had happened, ending with the incident with Uncle Al and the two students.

"Wild!" Bess's eyes went wide. "This Uncle Al sounds crazy to me. What do you think, Nan? Do you think he could be the one behind the threats? I mean anyone sending those notes has got to be a little crazy."

"I don't think the man's insane, Bess," Nancy said. "I do think he did overreact to those two guys fooling around. That doesn't make him crazy. Besides, what motive could he have that would make him send threats to the guests?"

"Okay, then we're back to Lisa." Bess nodded. "Because of what you said about the glider being sabotaged."

"She is still tops on my suspect list," Nancy said. "But there's more here than just a spoiled rich girl throwing what amounts to a glorified temper tantrum. What about Quinn's accident? And the attack on me?" Nancy pulled thoughtfully on a strand of hair. "If only I could talk to Quinn."

"Why not?" George asked. "Why don't you go to the hospital? It's not that far to Newport."

"I can't for one good reason. He's unconscious. He lapsed into a coma last night, and the doctor has no idea how long it'll be before he comes around—if ever."

"If ever?" Bess stared at her. "But that's horrible. That means Quinn could end up being the first real murder victim. Oh, I hope he doesn't die."

"I hope not either," Nancy replied. "For Marva's sake as well as his own." Then Nancy told Bess and George about the argument she'd overheard between Marva and Gil. "Marva swears Gil only yells at her because he loves her so much and he hates seeing her miserable. He really wants her to sell out and let someone else take over the problems—"

"Gil loves Marva?" Bess blurted out. "Oh, wow, is that a joke! The only person that guy loves is himself. He thinks he's God's gift to women. Haven't you noticed how he flirts with everyone? Just now as I was passing Lisa's cabin guess who I saw locked in a very serious kiss with Sara Lakin?"

"Gil?" Nancy and George both said at the same time.

"You got it. Mr. Wonderful, himself," Bess replied.

Nancy thoughtfully rubbed the side of her glass with her finger. "This case gets more complicated by the minute. Let's get going."

After lunch Nancy decided to pay a visit to Lisa Gregson. She wanted a chance to talk with the young woman—alone.

"I recognize you." Lisa smiled at Nancy as she opened the door. "You were there when I came to—after the crash."

"That's right." Nancy returned the smile. "I hope you're okay now."

"Oh, sure, I feel great." Lisa fiddled with the doorknob. "Do you want to come in?"

"Yes, I'd like to." Nancy stepped through the open door before Lisa could have a chance to change her mind. Crossing directly to a chair near the fireplace, Nancy sat down. "Actually I'd like to ask you a couple of questions about the accident. And about something else as well."

"By something else, do you mean the threat I got?" Lisa asked candidly as she sat down opposite Nancy. "Marva told me you'd want to question me about it. Did you happen to see my note?"

"Yours, and I saw Sara's picture and heard about Kirsten's tape."

"Brrr—" Lisa said. "Really creepy stuff, don't you think?" She shuddered involuntarily.

She's really upset about the death threat she received, Nancy thought. Or else she's a very good actress.

"I mean, who would want to do something like that? Other than Sara and Kirsten I don't know anyone here."

"I don't suppose you recognized the writing on the note?"

"No. It was only those three words. And it was printed."

"Probably someone trying to disguise his— or her—writing," Nancy said, watching for Lisa's reaction.

"Do you really think it could be a woman?" Lisa asked, slightly taken aback. "All this time I kept thinking it had to be a guy. I never thought about it being a woman. But I guess it is possible, huh?"

"There's no reason it couldn't be a woman." Nancy went on. "Now, about your accident. I have to be honest and tell you that because the damage to the glider is minor, I think you could have done it yourself. Especially because Sara made a comment that made me think you'd be capable of doing it."

"What?" Lisa's mouth dropped open and she stared at Nancy. "What are you talking about?"

Nancy explained that she knew that Lisa was having problems with her father. How she found out she kept to herself. "So, you can see how it looks to me, Lisa. Setting yourself up to have an accident is a good way to hurt your father."

"Oh, really! And what is Sara supposed to have said?" Lisa snapped.

"I don't want to cause trouble between you and your friend," Nancy apologized. "But when I asked Sara about your accident, she was evasive—she didn't want to talk at first. Then she said that if I knew you the way she does, I'd know the crash was no accident. So, you see, putting all that information together led me to believe—"

"Oh, you're so *wrong* it's not even funny!" Lisa yelled. She jumped up and began to pace the room. Then abruptly she stopped and balled her hands into fists before turning to face Nancy. "You're way off base, Nancy Drew. Yes, I hate my father. And I'd love to see him as unhappy as I am now. But there's no way I'm going to hurt myself in order to do that. You can trust me on that score, Ms. Detective."

"All right, Lisa." Nancy decided to back off a little. "I believe you." For some reason, she did. The girl's reactions seemed honest.

Lisa appeared to calm down and sat down opposite her again. "Look, I'm really scared about all this," she said. "And I want whoever is doing these horrible things caught. I promise I'll do anything I can to help. Whatever you want to know, I'll tell you."

"Good," Nancy said. That gave her an opening to ask Lisa about Sara and Gil.

"And about Sara's comment," Lisa went on before Nancy had a chance to ask. "Well, she was about as far off as you. And I don't understand that. She knows me, and should know I wouldn't do something stupid like crash my glider." Lisa shifted nervously on her chair. Nancy guessed she was deciding whether or not to say something more.

Nancy waited.

"Lisa," Nancy prodded. "There's more, isn't there? You can trust me."

A long pause followed before Lisa finally spoke. "The thing is, Sara's really not been

herself since we got here and she met Gil
Forrest. She has a huge crush on him. Every-
body knows he's engaged to Marva, but it
doesn't seem to matter to her. She's so jealous
I bet she blames *me* for letting him take me to
the infirmary."

"Hmmm . . ." What was with Gil, anyway?
Nancy wondered. If he really loved Marva,
what was he doing fooling around with Sara? If
he didn't, why was he pretending he did?
"Thanks for talking with me, Lisa." With a
smile, Nancy rose. "You've been a big help."

"Poor Sara," Bess said sympathetically after
Nancy told her what she'd learned. "I can
understand how she must feel. I've fallen for a
rat or two myself."

"I thought about it as I walked back here,"
Nancy said. "I think that Gil might have been
playing around with Sara because he was so
mad at Marva. He'd just had an argument with
her. If Sara's got a crush on him, the way Lisa
claims, and she happened to throw herself
at him at the right—or should I say
wrong—time . . . ?"

"I think you're being too nice," George
countered. "If a guy I was engaged to pulled a
stunt like that I'd never forgive him."

"I wonder how Marva would react if she
knew what was going on?" Bess speculated.

"I was wondering that, too," Nancy said.

But before I can solve Marva's problems, I need to figure out what Gil is up to, Nancy thought. And there's no better place to start than with Sara's other roommate.

Loud rock music blared from loudspeakers in the aerobics class where Nancy found Kirsten. A passing instructor had pointed her out to Nancy. "She's the tall one in yellow."

"Thanks." Nancy turned her attention to watching the naturally athletic girl. Kirsten's light brown hair was plaited into a single French braid that bounced against her back as she moved energetically to the final bars of the song.

Nancy watched as Kirsten walked toward the locker room, a towel draped around her neck.

"Excuse me, Kirsten." Nancy ran a couple of steps to stop the girl. "I'm Nancy Drew. Marva Phillips has asked me to look into the threats you and the others have been receiving. Would you mind talking to me for a few minutes?"

"If I can shower first," Kirsten replied easily. "I'm sweaty, and I don't want my muscles to stiffen."

Nancy quickly filled Kirsten in on the conversation she'd had with Lisa. The girls were standing in front of a mirror where Kirsten was replaiting her hair. "I don't enjoy prying into other people's private affairs, but I want to know what you think of Gil Forrest. Considering what is happening with Sara," Nancy added knowingly.

"Well, I agree with you about keeping my nose out of other people's business," Kirsten said, staring rather pointedly at Nancy in the mirror. "And I don't see how Gil's kissing Sara could be tied into the threats we got."

Kirsten stopped braiding a minute, thinking, her arms still up by her head. "There *is* something I do know about him, though, that might have some bearing on the threats. Now that I think about it, he *might* be the one sending them. I haven't told anyone about this, but I guess I'd better tell you." Kirsten dropped her arms and led Nancy to a quiet corner bench.

"What is it?" Nancy asked eagerly.

"Well, last week I went to Marva's office, looking for her, but only Gil was there. He looked really upset. He was holding a letter, and his hand was shaking. I don't know why I didn't just turn around and leave—you know, because he might have been embarrassed with me there—but I didn't. Something about the way he looked made me feel sorry for him. So I asked him if there was anything I could do."

"And?"

"Well, he obviously wanted to talk to someone." Kirsten shrugged. "And I happened to be there."

"Go on." Nancy felt she was on to the first real clue in the case.

"He showed me the letter he was holding. It was from a businessman, someone named Roger Coleman. This Coleman had made a really good offer to buy Marva out. I saw the figure on the letter, and it was a lot of money. Gil was upset because Marva had turned the offer down—cold."

"He actually told you all this?" Nancy asked.

"I know it sounds weird." Kirsten nodded. "I'm practically a stranger, and there he was telling me all that personal stuff. But he was so mad at Marva that he lost control. Maybe he was mad enough to send those threats to the guests. You know, to scare Marva into accepting Coleman's offer after all."

"Uh-huh," Nancy said, thinking. "Tell me, Kirsten, do you know anything about this Roger Coleman?"

"Just from pictures and reputation. He's a broker who goes around buying up businesses that are about to fail. I've heard my father mention him. My father's a business broker, too. But nothing like Coleman. Coleman has a reputation for being ruthless. He does whatever he has to to get what he wants." She stood up. "I really should get going."

"Of course," Nancy replied.

The two walked outside the complex together. A gray BMW was pulling up to the main building.

"I don't believe it!" Kirsten whispered to Nancy as the driver stepped out. "This is like ESP. We were just talking about him, and there he is. Roger Coleman himself."

Nancy watched as the man paused to glance around, spotted the two of them, and stepped over quickly.

Coleman was tall, with dark good looks. Probably in his late thirties, Nancy judged. Dressed in neatly pressed tan slacks, a plaid blue silk shirt open at the collar, with a well-tailored, raw silk sports jacket over it, he looked like the TV image of a go-getter tycoon.

"Afternoon, ladies." Coleman spoke in a low, pleasant voice with the hint of a western drawl. "I'm looking for Marva Phillips. Can you tell me where I might find her?"

"I'm not sure," Nancy said, "but she could be in her office." Coleman thanked her and left.

"What do you think, Nancy?" Kirsten asked with a backward glance at the businessman's retreating figure. "Do you think Marva's changed her mind and is going to sell? If she does, she's going to be a very rich woman."

And even if Gil Forrest doesn't love Marva, Nancy thought, if he marries her, wouldn't he be a very rich man?

Chapter

Nine

NANCY WAS WALKING AWAY from the main building, thinking about Gil and the offer to buy Club High Adventure, when Roger Coleman came back out the front door. Seeing Nancy, he waved and started talking.

"Well, Ms. Phillips wasn't in her office. I asked at the front desk if they knew where I could find her. Nothing! Zip!"

"Sorry," Nancy replied, adding a polite shrug. "I was only guessing."

"At least you tried to help. The person at the front desk just wanted me to leave my name. Said she'd let Marva know I'd been asking for her." He shook his head in disbelief. "Isn't that incredible?" He suddenly grinned good-naturedly at his own situation. "Where'd they think I dropped in from? Someplace down the street after a quick taxi ride? It took me close to forty minutes to drive here from the airport, most of it on that impossible cliff road."

"Forty minutes?" Nancy recalled the hour and a half drive she and her friends had made from Portland.

"Oh, not a commercial airport," he replied, seeing her confusion. "A little private strip up north of here. The closest one that'll accommodate a jet. I flew the Lear up from L.A." His explanation didn't even sound like bragging, Nancy thought. He said it the way anyone else would say he'd taken a bus.

Despite what Kirsten had told her about Coleman, Nancy found herself liking him. He was both easygoing and debonair.

"Was Marva expecting you, Mr.—uh—" Nancy didn't want to let on she knew his name.

"Now I'm the one being thoughtless. I'm Roger Coleman." He put out a capable-looking hand for her to shake.

"My name is Nancy Drew." She wasn't surprised by his firm grip. "Was Marva expecting you?" she repeated.

"I hope not." Coleman grinned. "I don't let people I'm doing business with know I'm coming. I like to pop in. Surprise 'em. I get better results that way."

"I have to admit I've heard of you, Mr. Coleman," Nancy said. "Now I think I understand how you earned your reputation."

"Please, call me Roger," he said in a warm tone. "Now, as for my reputation, I don't apologize for my ability to make money. Nothing wrong with that. Just as long as it's fair and profitable for everyone."

Nancy laughed at his candor. "Good enough," she agreed.

"And I've got to admit I know who you are, too. Just your name," he added. "Gil told me Marva was asking a Nancy Drew to help her with those threats. I hope you can get this mess cleared up before I become the new owner."

"From what I understand"—Nancy looked directly into his clear gray eyes—"Marva decided she's not going to sell."

"Oh, that was just her first answer. I never pay attention to first answers. At least not if it's a no." He looked around, as if appraising the club. "I've decided that I want to own this place. And I believe I have an offer she isn't going to refuse—if I can find her to make my offer."

Glancing over Coleman's shoulder, Nancy said, "I think you're about to have the chance. Here she is now."

The club's green van had pulled up behind

the BMW. Marva and Gil got out. Nancy noticed that Gil didn't seem even vaguely surprised to see Coleman. In fact, his expression told her that he was not only happy to see the businessman, but might actually have been expecting him. As for Marva, the grim set of her features was evidence enough that she wasn't happy to find Roger Coleman on her property.

As the two came toward Nancy and Coleman, they had a quick exchange of words. Gil was saying something to which Marva was emphatically shaking her head no. But a second later he stopped and touched her arm. She nodded yes this time.

Gil was the first to speak, suggesting cool drinks at a quiet poolside table. He invited Nancy to join them.

"Thanks, but I'll pass," Nancy replied. "If you're not going to use your office for a while, Marva, I'd like to go over those files we discussed."

While Gil, Marva, and Coleman went off, Nancy headed for Marva's office. It took her only a short while to locate the personnel records. After pulling the folders, she sat down at Marva's desk, stacking the files next to her.

She read through the files of everyone, even part-time clerical help. She couldn't eliminate anyone. The lengthy application forms included letters of reference, résumés, health insurance forms, and miscellaneous letters and notes. Nothing seemed out of place in any of them. With a sigh, Nancy closed the cover of the folder belonging to Uncle Al and set it on top of the tall pile she'd already finished.

After rubbing her tired eyes, she reached up and stretched. She'd been at it for two hours and absolutely nothing had come of it.

One more to go. With a sigh, Nancy opened the folder and began to read.

Five minutes later she closed the cover, nodding once to herself. She'd actually found something that might just relate to the case.

Getting to her feet, Nancy began to pace— and think. She suddenly realized she hadn't known much about Gil Forrest before reading his file, only the few things Marva had told her about him.

The two had met on a bicycle tour of Europe when they were in college. Marva had gone to Oregon State, while Gil had attended college in the Midwest. Apparently, Gil had approached Marva a year earlier and asked her for a job, and she had offered him the one as her assistant.

But it was what had happened in Gil's life between their first meeting and his coming to work for Marva that was so intriguing. It was all there in his files.

Nancy sat down again and picked up Gil's folder. His résumé showed that after graduating with a degree in business administration, Gil had moved to Seattle, where he'd gotten his real estate broker's license. He'd gone to work for a large firm, dealing in luxury resort property. With his good looks and persuasive personality, he must have cleaned up, Nancy decided. Why had he made the switch from a fast-paced existence in a large city like Seattle to a life of teaching hang gliding here in the wilderness?

Maybe that was why Gil was so interested in Roger Coleman's offer. If Marva accepted and they married, he'd have access to all that money. Maybe he wanted to get back on the fast track and become a tycoon like Coleman. Marva's money would be his bankroll. It was certainly a strong enough motive if, indeed, it turned out that Gil was behind the threats.

Satisfied that she'd learned as much as she could from the files, Nancy left the office, turning out the light and making sure the door was locked. She didn't hear the footsteps moving quietly behind her. Suddenly her vision was cut off as a hood was pulled over her head.

Nancy tried to scream, but a hand covered her face, shoving the coarse material against her nose and into her mouth. Barely able to breathe, she felt herself being dragged down the hall.

Just as suddenly, the hand was gone from her face. Nancy was pushed against a cold, hard wall. She lost her balance, stumbling to her knees.

With a sense of foreboding, she heard the slam of a metal door behind her. Then a lock clicked home.

Nancy pulled the hood from her head. Her heart sank when she realized what had happened. Someone had thrown her into the kitchen's huge, deep freezer. And she was locked in!

Chapter

Ten

NANCY STARED at the heavy door, which was white with frost. Her first thought was to unlock the door, then get out and chase down her attacker.

Almost instantly, she remembered what Marva had said about the freezer door needing to be fixed. The inside latch was broken. Anyone unlucky enough to be inside when the door was closed would be trapped. At least until someone came along and opened it from the outside. And no one would hear her screams since the thick-walled room was soundproof. No doubt her attacker was well aware of these facts.

How long could she be trapped before someone discovered her in there? Any amount of
time could be too long, Nancy realized as she
felt the cold settle around her.

With sudden dread Nancy remembered the
dinner dance that night wasn't taking place
until nine o'clock! That meant that a lot of the
crew wouldn't even be on duty yet. Nancy
could freeze to death long before anyone came
and found her.

A shiver ran up her spine—not from fright,
but from cold. Her light cotton slacks and knit
shirt were no protection from the damp, frigid
air. She rubbed at her arms to try to warm
them as she looked for something—anything
—that would help her escape.

Nancy was thankful for one thing—
the freezer light didn't automatically go out
when the door was shut. It would have
been even worse if she'd been locked in the
dark.

Maybe she could find something she could
use to jimmy the lock open. Nancy quickly
inspected the contents of the freezer. But there
was nothing she could use to escape with. Only
rows of shelves with neatly stacked boxes of
vegetables and wrapped foil packages—probably cuts of meat.

Two sides of beef hung at the back of the
small room. She studied the hooks they were
suspended from. Was there any way she could

use them? Not a chance, she decided, turning her attention back to the shelves.

With a hand that was beginning to shake from the cold, she picked up one of the rectangular foil packages. It was rock hard, shaped almost like a brick. What if she pounded on the door with it? Surely someone would hear her if she beat on it long enough.

But that was the problem. How long could she hold out? How long would it be before anyone heard her? The freezer was in a hall behind the kitchen, all by itself. No one would come back there unless they specifically wanted to get into the freezer.

Discouraged, she was about to put the package back on the shelf, when her gaze fell on a small round dial near the door. The thermostat. It gave a temperature reading of zero degrees. Nancy remembered something she'd learned about freezers—the door will automatically unlock if the thermostat stops working.

All I need to do is make sure it's not working, she thought, with sudden hope. And I have the perfect weapon right here in my hand to make sure it's not.

Moving quickly to the thermostat, she lifted the frozen package and hit the glass cover of the dial hard. It didn't crack. Apparently the glass was thicker than she'd judged. Throwing her weight into it, she hit the dial again. Still nothing. Frustrated, Nancy began hammering at it. By now her numbed fingers were barely working and her hand was beginning to stick to the frozen package.

It took several more hits before the glass on the thermostat suddenly shattered in several places at once. Listening carefully, Nancy heard a muffled click as the outside lock was released. She was free!

George and Bess were both ready to leave the cabin by the time Nancy returned. But after one look at her, the other girls demanded to know what had happened.

"I definitely don't like it," George said, after Nancy had told them about her time in the freezer. "This makes twice someone has tried to kill you. And we have no idea who could be responsible. It's no secret what you're doing here. The entire staff knows, and most of the guests. Don't you think it's time to call the police?"

"I agree," Bess said, putting her hand on Nancy's. "This thing isn't worth risking your life for."

"I admit it's dangerous," Nancy said, "but

that must be because I'm getting close to the answer. Besides, I promised Marva I wouldn't call in the police yet."

"Didn't the doctor have to report Larry Quinn's accident?" Bess wanted to know.

"No. Because it was just that—an accident. There was no foul play as far as anyone knew." She assured her friends that she'd be more careful and would stay on the alert from then on.

"You promise?" Bess said.

Nancy gave a decisive nod of her head. It was only then that it dawned on her that her two friends were already dressed for the dance that night. "Is it that late already?" she asked. "I thought dinner wasn't going to be until late."

"Oh, it's not," Bess replied. "But there's some early entertainment planned out by the pool. George and I thought we'd go over."

"But we won't now," George added quickly. "We'll stay here with you."

"Don't be silly," Nancy said. "You don't have to baby-sit me. You guys go ahead. I'll be fine. In fact I think I'll take a nice long, hot bath and thaw out. I feel a little like some of those slabs of beef in the freezer." She gave a little laugh.

"Well . . ." George hesitated.

"Go. Please." Nancy smiled. "Actually, you can do a little sleuthing for me."

"Like what?" Bess asked.

"I'd like you two to keep your eyes open. Notice if anyone acts strange. You know, if someone's where he shouldn't be—that sort of thing."

"You got it," George promised.

"And don't be too long," Bess added as they were leaving. "Or we'll start worrying and come back for you."

Remembering that locked doors were no barrier to a determined criminal, Nancy propped a chair under the knob before she relaxed into her scented bath bubbles. She focused her thoughts and went over what she knew of the case so far.

Lisa Gregson was no longer a suspect as far as Nancy was concerned. Nancy was convinced that Lisa's problems had nothing to do with the club crime.

Sara Lakin had a serious crush on Gil, or so Lisa said. That was backed up by what Bess had seen. Though that might make Sara want to see Marva have problems with Club High Adventure, Nancy could not picture the high-strung brunette carrying out any of the recent attacks.

As for Kirsten, she was athletic and

probably strong enough to have pushed Nancy over the railing of Quinn's cabin and dragged her into the freezer, but she had no motive.

Marva's original thought still offered the strongest motive: that someone was out to destroy the club's reputation, probably to get Marva to sell out. The obvious people who came to mind were Marva's fiancé, Gil, and Roger Coleman.

Although Nancy found the wealthy tycoon charming and friendly, he did have a reputation for being ruthless in business. And even though he'd just arrived that afternoon, he could easily have had someone working for him.

Could that someone be Gil? There could be a tie-in between the two men. Gil had been a real estate broker before coming to work for Marva. He'd dealt with expensive properties, and Roger Coleman's occupation was buying up expensive properties.

Gil had access to the cabins and other areas of the club. That was important. Also, he would have known about such inside details as the broken freezer door.

There had to be something she was missing. Some connection.

I'd better hurry up and find out what it is, Nancy thought. Because whoever started out only making threats was now taking serious risks.

"Risks that are putting your own life in danger, Nancy Drew," she said to herself.

There'd been two attempts on her life already. The next one could very well prove fatal.

Chapter

Eleven

NANCY PAUSED in front of the bedroom mirror for a last-minute check. Partly to take her mind off the frustrations of the case, she'd put on one of her favorite outfits—a full flowered skirt teamed with a pale green scoopneck top. The green set off the red-gold highlights in her hair.

Satisfied, she slipped her feet into high-heeled sandals, picked up her light cotton sweater from the bed and left the cabin.

Dinner was just being served when Nancy entered the dining room. She slid into her chair as a waiter was putting an iced fruit cup at her place. Nancy smiled hello at Bess and

George and at the other five guests at their table.

The normally casual dining room had been transformed into a romantic fantasyland. Blue linen cloths covered the otherwise utilitarian pine tables, and arrangements of wildflowers and baby's breath sat in the center of each table.

"Great, isn't it?" Bess said happily. "And did you notice? There's going to be a live band." She nodded in the direction of the French doors that ran the length of the dining room and overlooked the pool and veranda.

Nancy turned to look and saw two young men in matching silver jackets checking the sound system, while another band member removed a guitar from its case. "Hope they're good," she commented, when a movement in the shadows on the veranda caught her eyes.

It was Roger Coleman, talking animatedly with Al Hunt. Why was Coleman still here? Nancy wondered. Considering the cool reception he'd received from Marva that afternoon, he should have been back in Los Angeles by now. Also, what was he doing having an engrossing conversation with the rock-climbing instructor?

Intrigued, Nancy shoved her chair back and stood up. "I see something I want to check out. Be right back," she said in an undertone to Bess and George, and hurried from the room.

Bess looked at George. "Where do you suppose Nancy's headed?"

George shot a worried look after Nancy. "I wonder if we should go after her? I mean with all that's been going on, I'm not sure we should let her go off by herself."

"I agree," Bess said. "But wouldn't it look kind of funny if we all went rushing out? It might just draw the wrong person's attention."

"You're right." George nodded. "Nancy should know what she's doing. But if she's not back in five minutes, I vote we go after her."

Nancy had wound her way through the maze of tables to the far end of the room where the French doors opened onto the veranda. By the time she'd made it outside, however, the two men were no longer in sight. Too bad. She'd really wanted to overhear what they'd been saying. She promised herself to keep an eye out for them.

As people finished eating, they drifted from the dining room out onto the veranda. The band had begun to play some light rock as background music. Bess and George had gone down to the end of the pool to get closer.

Nancy stayed by herself, lying back on the chaise longue and enjoying the rich velvet sky punctuated with millions of tiny stars.

"Beautiful, don't you think?" a warm masculine voice said from close behind her shoulder, startling her.

"Oh, Mr. Coleman—" Nancy sat up quickly. "Hello!"

"Roger—please." He smiled as he sat down beside her. "I thought we were on a first-name basis."

"I'm curious—Roger," Nancy said. "I was wondering why you're still here."

"You mean you expected Marva to demand that I leave and not come back? That would have been a little dramatic, don't you think? Actually we got along quite nicely when we talked this afternoon. I think we understand each other."

"You do?" Nancy asked. It hadn't looked that way to her. Things must have changed after she left.

"Yes. Marva kindly suggested I stay the night and get an early start in the morning. Seems at this time of the year, the fog comes up off the ocean early and banks against the cliff. Driving on the coast road can be rather dangerous." The corners of his mouth lifted in a wry smile. "I suppose she didn't want to think about going to sleep and waking up tomorrow morning to find out I'd been killed."

Standing, Coleman put out his hand. "The band seems to have switched over to the kind

of dance music my feet understand. Shall we?"
Nancy agreed. What better chance to keep an
eye on him?

They hadn't been dancing long before one of
the guys from her hang-gliding class cut in on
them. She lost track of Coleman as she danced
with several other young men.

Then, after two or three more numbers,
Nancy found herself in Gil Forrest's arms.

"Having a good time?" he asked politely.

"Yes, thank you," she replied, but she was
feeling distinctly uncomfortable dancing with
him, considering what she now knew about
him.

"I wanted to talk to you alone," he said,
moving skillfully to the beat of a slow dance.
"This seemed to be as good a way as any."

"Does that mean you don't want Marva to
hear what you have to say to me?"

He nodded. "I decided to tell you exactly
where I'm coming from. That way, maybe, you
won't go snooping around and foul up my
relationship with Marva. Maybe you won't tell
her things that would only hurt her. After all,
I'm not perfect. No one is. But that doesn't
make me a crook."

"Where exactly *are* you coming from, Gil?"
Nancy tilted her head so she could look directly into his eyes.

"I admit I want Marva to sell the club to
Coleman. She doesn't need all the grief the

club's been giving her lately. And Coleman's offer is far too good to pass up. It would make her a wealthy woman."

"Which in turn would give you access to a lot of money," Nancy concluded, giving him a hard look. It was as good a time as any to test her theory.

"Yes. It would," Gil replied evenly. "I'd be dishonest if I said I didn't care about money. I do. But I want you to know I love Marva. Money or no money."

The music ended, and Gil thanked Nancy for the dance. She couldn't dismiss from her mind the fact that Gil still had one of the strongest motives of any suspect on her list. But he had sought her out to try to make his position clear. If he were behind the threats, would he be so open about his feelings?

As Nancy was trying to work out the logic behind Gil's behavior, Marva appeared.

"I was watching you dance with Gil," she said. There was a troubled expression in her deep blue eyes. "What were you two talking about? You looked so serious."

Nancy hesitated. How much of what Gil had said was really necessary to pass on to Marva?

"He wanted to convince me that although he is all for you giving up this club," she said, choosing her words carefully, "he would never do anything drastic—like sending those threats to scare you into selling out."

"Poor Gil. I hope he doesn't think I suspect that." She jerked her head toward Nancy. "You don't think that, do you? Because that would be ridiculous. Gil loves me."

"Yes," Nancy said kindly. "He told me that, too."

"Nancy, I know that Gil's behavior hasn't been the best lately. But I wish you'd put it down to the strain we're all under—" Marva paused, and a puzzled expression came over her face.

Nancy followed Marva's eyes and saw that she was staring toward the main building.

"What is it, Marva?" Nancy asked.

"Something very strange," Marva answered. "There's a light on in my office." She turned to Nancy. "I was in there only a while ago, making a phone call. I distinctly remember shutting off the light as I left. And I also remember locking the door."

"Could it be Gil?" Nancy asked.

"Uh-uh." Marva shook her head firmly. "I know where Gil is. He wanted to do some last-minute work on a couple of the gliders before tomorrow's class. He's in the work-room."

"Then I think we'd better investigate." Nancy jumped up. She called out to George that they were going to Marva's office.

It took only a few minutes for the two to

enter the building and make their way down the hall toward Marva's office.

While they were still only a few feet away from the door, Nancy held up her hand to stop Marva. "The light's out now," she said in a whisper, pointing to the dark crack at the bottom of the door. "Whoever was in there has probably gone. But maybe not. Let me go first."

Slipping out of her high heels, Nancy picked one up and held it with the sharp heel pointing out. Good weapon in case I have to defend myself, Nancy thought. Then she crept the last few feet toward the closed door. Putting her hand on the knob, she turned it and pushed the door open at the same time. She reached in to snap on the light.

"Oh no!" Nancy gasped as the light flooded the room, showing papers strewn everywhere, furniture knocked over, and shards of broken glass littering the floor.

Someone had ransacked the place.

Chapter

Twelve

Nancy, what is it?" Marva cried out. Rushing to the open doorway to stand beside Nancy, she stared into her office, but didn't move. "Who could have done this?"

"What I'd like to know is *why?*" Nancy asked as she entered the room and stepped over the papers that had been scattered everywhere from the open file drawers.

She bent to retrieve some that were lying just in front of her. As she straightened up, Nancy glanced at the wall over the couch. Marva had a collection of framed photos hanging there—mementos of past club guests, famous people who'd visited the club, friends, and family. It wasn't these Nancy saw. Her eyes were drawn to a pale square on the wall where a photo had been but wasn't now.

"Marva." Nancy turned to face her. "Did you take a photo off this wall recently? I think one is missing."

"Excuse me?" Marva looked up from the mess to the wall. "No, I didn't. Someone else must have taken it down." A frown creased her forehead. "You don't suppose it was the person who broke in, do you?" Marva asked, puzzled. "It was just an old photo of my father."

"Your father?"

"Yes—well, not only my father. I was in it, too. Along with some of the guests who were here that day."

"Do you have another print?"

"No, I don't think so." The loss was just beginning to sink in. "Oh, Nancy, I don't even have the negative. I'll never be able to replace it. And it was a favorite of mine." Marva looked wistfully at the spot where the photo had been.

"Marva, tell me—those guests, can you remember who they were? What did the photo look like? Exactly."

"Let me think. . . ." Marva leaned against the desk and tried to remember. Finally she raised her head to look at Nancy.

"Strange, isn't it, how you can look at something every day, but then, when it's gone, you have trouble remembering the details?"

"I know." Nancy nodded her agreement. "But please try. I have a feeling it's important."

"Basically it was a picture of my father, taken when I was about seven. My father and I and a group of guests went hiking up to Devil's Rock. Someone took a photograph of all of us when we got to the top."

Nancy thought for a moment. "Do you remember anything else about the photograph? Who in particular might have been in the group?"

Marva shook her head. "You know—at that age all the guests were just so many adults to me. In the photo, they were just figures in the background. I never really paid much attention to them. Sorry, Nancy."

"It's okay," Nancy said. "Maybe the photo will turn up," she added. She gestured to the papers Marva had been clutching in her hand. "Can you tell what papers are missing?"

"Oh, it's impossible," Marva said, waving them in frustration. "I'll have to spend hours sorting them out. But I did notice one thing. This empty file folder is one I kept on Roger Coleman's offer to buy the club."

"Hello," a male voice sung out.

At the sound of the voice, both Nancy and

Marva swung about to see Roger Coleman standing in the open doorway.

"I saw the light on in here and thought I might catch you before you went—" He broke off to stare at the wrecked office. "What happened here?"

"A break-in, obviously," Nancy replied.

"So I see. Someone certainly did a thorough job," Coleman commented.

"What was it you wanted to see me about, Roger?" Marva spoke up.

"I thought we might have another chat. Since I plan to leave first thing tomorrow morning, I knew there wouldn't be time then. Just a few minutes. *Alone,*" he said emphatically, with a polite smile in Nancy's direction.

"This is hardly the time for a business talk," Nancy said, feeling protective of Marva.

"That's all right, Nancy," Marva told her. "Actually, this might be the perfect time for Roger and me to talk."

Nancy was reluctant to leave. But it was apparent that the two of them wanted privacy.

When she walked out of the building, she found Bess and George waiting for her. The band had left, and only a few stragglers from the party hung about, chatting by the pool.

"Hi!" Bess linked her arm in Nancy's. "We knew you were in talking to Marva and decided to wait."

"We thought it would be better if we all walked back to the cabin together. Safety in numbers, you know," George said.

"What would I do without you guys?" Nancy linked her arm with George's. "I want to hear anything you have to report about the party, and then I'm going to fill you in on the latest with Marva."

Bess reached for another cookie. Dipping it into her milk, she paused before bringing it to her mouth. "So I guess I'm a failure as a spy. I didn't learn a single thing that might help, Nan. Sorry."

The three were curled up on the couches in the cabin, a nearly empty package of cookies on the coffee table. A cozy fire crackled in the fireplace, taking the night chill out of the air.

"Ditto for me," George said. "What do you suppose anyone wanted with the papers on Coleman's offer?"

"I'm not sure," Nancy said. "But I can't help thinking his showing up just at that moment, right after we found the office ransacked, was too well-timed."

"You mean he might have been the one who did it?" George asked.

"Or he hired someone to break in for him," Nancy said. "Maybe he was hanging around waiting for Marva to discover the chaos. Maybe he hoped she'd be so upset that she'd cave in and sell him the club."

Nancy put an unfinished cookie down on her napkin. "Of course Gil might have done it. Marva said that he'd told her he was going to the workroom, but that could have been a lie. It could even have been Uncle Al." Nancy explained that she'd seen Coleman in deep conversation with the climbing instructor. "He could work for Coleman."

"Okay. So it all seems to come down to Coleman," George said in a positive tone.

"But Nancy told us how nice he is," Bess argued.

"Bess, how many times has Nancy been involved with a criminal who *seemed* nice at the start, then ended up being a pure rat?" George asked.

"Okay. Coleman's the bad guy." Bess tried to stifle a yawn, then gave up. "Case solved. I'm going to bed." She stood up and stretched. "See you guys in the morning. Good night."

"Hold on a minute, Bess." Nancy stood up. "You're going to have to put off bed for a little while. Right now, I need you to come with me."

Nancy handed her two friends their sweaters and started to lead them toward the front door.

"Where are we going?" George asked.

"I want to take a look in Uncle Al's cabin. Maybe I'll be able to find something that will tell me if he's working for Coleman," Nancy said, ignoring Bess's sleepy protest. "Let's go, you two."

There was a light showing through the blinds as they approached the cabin. George touched Nancy's arm. "He's in there. We can't break in now."

"Not necessarily," Nancy replied in a low voice. "Maybe he left the light on. Wait here, I'll check."

A couple of minutes later Nancy was standing on the porch motioning to her friends. "Just as I thought," she whispered when they had joined her. "It's only a night light." Nancy soon had the door open.

"If anything, this guy is too neat," George complained after the three had searched through the cabin. She stood in the center of the living room, hands on hips. "This place is like a motel room. I can't believe anyone really lives here."

"You're right," Nancy agreed. "There's nothing personal here. No plants, no books or magazines, no photos or letters."

"You're wrong about photos." Bess spoke up from where she knelt by the fireplace, poking through the ashes. "Crazy. But he seems to prefer burning them."

"What do you mean?" Nancy hurried over to Bess's side. Kneeling, she reached in and pulled out a partially burned photo.

The half that was left showed a kind-looking man, his arm out, holding hands with someone. The seven-year-old Marva, Nancy guessed, but she couldn't be sure because all that was left of the little girl was a small, slender arm and the tiniest glimpse of a kid's sneaker. In the background some hikers were sitting and resting, their faces mainly out-of-focus blurs.

Nancy handed it to Bess and George. "I'll bet you anything this is the photo that was taken from Marva's office tonight," she said. "But why would Uncle Al want to destroy this old picture?" she asked, almost to herself. It just didn't make any sense.

"Isn't that the trail to the top of Devil's Rock?" George asked, tapping the photo with her finger.

"Probably. Marva did say that's where it was taken," Nancy answered, looking at the photo again.

"Hmmm—maybe Uncle Al's got a thing about that place," Bess joked. "You know, Devil's Rock. Evil stuff. All that."

"Bess, this isn't the time to be—"

"I don't think it's smart for us to hang around here much longer," Nancy inter-

115

rupted. "This photo's only half burned. Maybe Al was in the middle of destroying it. Which means he might be on his way back right—"

A heavy tread made the front porch creak. All three girls turned toward the sound and held their breath. Three more steps in quick succession proved for certain that Al Hunt had returned.

Chapter

Thirteen

NANCY POINTED. George was the first to follow her direction and move toward the bedroom and the low window to safety outside. Bess, her eyes round and staring, was rooted to her spot, but she finally budged when she heard the jingle of keys.

Nancy was right behind Bess on her dash to the bedroom. At the last second she veered off and darted into the open kitchen directly opposite the front door.

She dove for cover behind the counter just as she saw Al Hunt standing framed in the doorway. Since he didn't make a move toward her, Nancy could only guess he hadn't seen her.

It was foolish to stay, but she had to have a solid piece of evidence. Still hunkering low, Nancy saw what she needed—a glass on top of the counter beside the sink.

Before she could grab it, Nancy saw Al's feet moving toward her. Nancy was ready for him. He might have the advantage of size, but she had the advantage of surprise.

Nancy held her breath, waiting for the right moment. Several seconds passed. Nancy kept her eyes on Al's feet from around a corner of the counter. Then, for some reason, Al stopped short of the counter and turned toward the fireplace.

Peering out from behind the counter, Nancy watched as he picked up the poker and disturbed the ashes. Checking to make sure the picture was all burned, Nancy thought. Satisfied that it was destroyed, Al headed for the bedroom.

When she saw he had closed the bedroom door, Nancy darted back across the kitchen floor and snaked her hand up to retrieve the solitary glass.

Still keeping an eye on the bedroom door, Nancy walked softly across the living room, casting one last look at the fireplace. There was a lot about Al Hunt she didn't know, Nancy thought as she silently let herself out the front door.

Once outside, she stared at the glass in her hand. With any luck there'll be some good prints on this, she thought as she looked around for Bess and George.

"There you are," she heard Bess whispering from the darkness. "Over here."

Nancy's eyes adjusted to the night and she turned to where she'd heard Bess's voice. Then, out of nowhere, George appeared at her side.

Nancy grabbed on to George and dragged her over to where she'd heard Bess's voice coming from. The three of them quickly stole away from Al's cabin.

"Excuse me for asking," George said to Nancy when they were a safe distance away and heading toward their own cabin, "but we're out in the boonies, here, remember. Just where are you planning to have those fingerprints checked?"

"Tomorrow morning we'll take them into Portland," she said.

"We?" Bess asked. "Listen, Nancy, after tonight's little escapade, I'm not sure I like this case." Bess had been chattering the whole way back from Hunt's cabin about what could have happened if they'd been caught.

"Calm down, Bess," George said. "Nancy

needs our help, and she's going to get it. Besides, what can happen in Portland, far away from Club High Adventure?"

Bess rolled her eyes, then sighed. "I guess you're right."

"That's the spirit," Nancy said, laughing.

They had reached their cabin. "I think we should all get a good night's sleep," Nancy said, yawning. "We need to be as alert as possible for what we have to do tomorrow. See you in the morning."

"All right, now give." Bess wadded up the wrapper from her sausage-and-biscuit breakfast sandwich and stuffed it into the jeep's litter bag as they roared down the highway toward Portland. "I'm ready to listen."

"Me, too," George said, gulping the last of her orange juice.

"I didn't realize what the case was really about until we found that photo in Uncle Al's cabin."

"But why do George and I have to go to Portland with you?" Bess had dug into her tote and was now putting on fresh lip gloss. "It doesn't take three of us to take a set of prints to the police."

"I'm going to drop you two at the library. I'd like you to read old newspaper stories from the time that Marva's mystery photo was taken.

Since Marva was about seven, that would make it eighteen years ago."

"What are we looking for?" George asked.

"A link. Anything that might have happened at the club eighteen years ago to make Al Hunt destroy a picture," Nancy explained.

"I don't get it," Bess complained. "What link could there possibly be?"

"I think it can involve only one person. Only one person has been connected with the club for the past eighteen years."

"Marva!" Bess gasped. "But what's the link? You can't believe she's behind these attempts on people's lives."

"No, I honestly don't think that, Bess." Frustrated, Nancy drummed her fingers against the steering wheel. "I don't know what to think."

"What about Larry Quinn?" George asked. "Do you think he might know who tried to kill him?"

"I don't think so," Nancy said. "I'm pretty sure he did consider his threat as only a childish hoax."

"Someone did try to kill him," George pointed out.

"But it wasn't necessarily Quinn that the killer was trying for. He should never have been on that trail in the first place. Uncle Al told me that trail is only for staff members and guests if they're with a staff member. Marva was right behind Quinn when he had his accident—"

"Which could mean that the *accident* might have really been meant for a staff member. It might have been set for Marva," George concluded, thinking out loud.

Bess spoke up excitedly. "Also, Marva likes to hang glide. So Lisa's accident could have been meant for Marva, too."

"And then again . . ." Nancy shrugged. "It could all be a smokescreen. I don't know. There are still too many unanswered questions."

Once they arrived in Portland, Nancy dropped Bess and George at the public library, then drove to the police station. She had called that morning and spoken to Detective Claudia O'Keefe, describing what she needed and giving her father as a reference.

Inside the one-story building, Nancy told the desk sergeant who she was and almost instantly an attractive, auburn-haired woman in her early thirties came out to greet her.

"It's a pleasure to meet you," O'Keefe said, shaking Nancy's hand. "Chief McGinnis back in River Heights said you're quite a detective."

Nancy smiled. "Well, I've solved a few

cases." She handed O'Keefe the glass she had found in Hunt's cabin. "Here's the evidence I told you about."

"Let's hope we can get to the bottom of what's happening up at Club High Adventure," O'Keefe said, taking the glass. "I just wish Ms. Phillips had asked for our help earlier. But better late than never. Come back later and I'll let you know what, if anything, I've been able to come up with."

Nancy thanked O'Keefe and left the station to help Bess and George in their search at the library.

"I've had it," Bess complained wearily, an hour after Nancy had met them at the microfilm readers. "I've skimmed so many articles my eyes are crossed."

"I'm ready to call it quits, too," George said, looking up. "I haven't run across a single . . . Wait a minute," she cried loud enough to annoy three people at a nearby table. "Nan, I think I've found something."

George pointed at the screen on which a portion of a newspaper page was projected. "Take a look at that."

Nancy's eyes scanned the article. Then she read the fine print under a headline. "Eighteen years ago this month," she said, thinking out loud.

"What is it, Nancy?" Bess asked, leaning over Nancy's shoulder.

"Something that can't be just a coincidence, Bess," Nancy said, and she read the caption out loud:

"'Gruesome Murder at Club High Adventure, on Top of Deadly Devil's Rock.'"

Chapter

Fourteen

BESS BENT OVER her friend's shoulder to get a better look at the microfilm screen.

George slid out of the chair, letting Nancy take her place. "Here, sit down, you can see better."

After skimming the first few lines again, Nancy began excitedly to read the story aloud.

Seattle computer entrepreneur E. Raymond Jensen was killed in a 190-foot fall yesterday morning during an ascent of Devil's Rock, a popular climber's landmark eighteen miles south of Newport. Jensen's business partner, Alden Hunsfield, has been arrested on suspicion of murder. The 43-year-old entrepreneur may have been pushed to his death.

Lincoln County Sheriff's deputies have Hunsfield, of Britebyte Corporation, in custody. The two men had been vacationing at Club High Adventure, a luxury resort catering to lovers of risky sports.

An eyewitness to the fall was the club owner's seven-year-old daughter, whose name is currently being withheld.

"If the little girl hadn't seen the whole thing, we would have written this off as just another climbing accident," Sheriff Mike Parker said.

Jensen and Hunsfield were scaling the final cliff face before the summit when the young witness says she saw Hunsfield loosen a piton holding his partner's safety line. Hunsfield, according to the girl, then attacked Jensen, causing the victim to plummet to a ledge nearly 200 feet below.

Hunsfield has denied the charges, claiming that the piton was coming loose under the strain of Jensen's weight and that he was trying to save the man when he fell.

"Marva Phillips!" George and Bess chorused in unison. "The little girl was Marva."

"It says here that the murderer's name was

Alden Hunsfield," Nancy added. "Does that sound familiar? Alden Hunsfield and Al Hunt sound too much alike to be a coincidence."

Quickly Nancy wound the microfilm forward. "There's got to be more on this. Something about the trial. What happened—" The spool of film had ended.

"Here—this is the next one in order," George said, yanking a spool from the pile beside the machine.

Nancy inserted the new spool, and the three friends leaned forward. "Here's something," Nancy exclaimed. "This article mentions the results of the trial. Hunsfield was convicted of murder, but the charge was reduced to second-degree. Which means he could be paroled by now."

"But if Uncle Al's really this Alden Hunsfield, what's he doing back at the camp?" Bess wanted to know. "That's really stupid."

"Haven't you heard?" George answered her. "The criminal always returns to the scene of the crime."

"Only if he's got unfinished business," Nancy said in a grim voice. "If Hunsfield is Hunt, he's at the club for only one reason. To get revenge against the one witness who sent him to jail. And that explains why he burned the photo—he and his partner must have been in it." She leapt up. "There's one way to know if the two men are one and the same."

"The fingerprints," George cried out.

"Right!" Nancy grabbed her purse. "Come on. Back to the police station."

Nancy left Bess and George in the car as she hurried inside to see Detective O'Keefe.

"Hope this information helps. It came in over the FAX line from Washington, D.C., just a few minutes ago," O'Keefe said, handing Nancy the report.

Nancy glanced over the sheet of paper and nodded grimly. "I think you'd better get some officers up to Club High Adventure—fast. This man is a murderer, and I think he's about to become one again." She filled O'Keefe in on the details.

The detective agreed with Nancy's theory and told Nancy she'd have several cars on their way immediately.

"The prints matched," Nancy said to Bess and George as she climbed into the driver's seat of the jeep a few minutes later. "There's no doubt. Uncle Al is Hunsfield."

"Nancy," George said. "I just remembered. Al's taking a class of advanced climbers up Devil's Rock this afternoon, and I heard Marva say she was going to join them."

"When is the class?" Nancy asked, shooting a glance at her watch. "It's one-forty now."

"Oh no!" George exclaimed. "The class is supposed to leave the clubhouse at three.

That's only an hour and twenty minutes from now."

"But it's an hour-and-a-half drive back to the club," Bess said, her eyes wide in despair. "We'll never make it back in time."

Nancy reached for the ignition key and switched it on.

"We have to," she said, quickly throwing the jeep into gear. "It's the only way we're going to stop a second murder from taking place on Devil's Rock!"

Chapter

Fifteen

EVERYTHING'S CLEAR NOW. Marva's been Al's intended victim all along," Nancy said, pulling away from the police station.

"Do you think we can make it?" George asked, worried. "Most of the trip is along that mountain-coast road. And we can go only so fast."

"Don't forget those awful rocky cliffs," Bess moaned. "Isn't there a different road we can take? Something quicker? Something safer? Like this nice, wide freeway?" She made a grab for the metal roll bar as Nancy whipped the jeep up the on-ramp and into the afternoon traffic.

"I wish we could," Nancy called over to Bess, the wind stirring her hair around her face as she maneuvered the jeep into the fast lane. "But there's only one way to get back—the coast road."

"Do me a favor, Nancy," Bess shouted over the rush of wind. "Make your next case one back in good old River Heights. It's safer there."

Forty minutes later Nancy left the westbound freeway to take the winding mountain road over which they'd driven hours earlier.

The road dipped and climbed, swung back and forth in sharp curves as it followed the natural line of the terrain. Fortunately the jeep was the perfect vehicle for rough driving, and Nancy handled it expertly. The road was nearly deserted. Encountering an occasional slow-moving log truck, its long trailer loaded with huge redwood trunks, Nancy would bear down on the horn until the driver pulled over enough to let them slip by.

"We've got to be near the coast road by now," George said with an anxious glance at her watch. "We don't have much time to get there. We're really cutting it close."

"I think I can smell the ocean," Bess said in a hopeful voice. "I remember that huge grove of pine trees up there on that ridge." She pointed to a sharply rising hill just in front of them. "Look, Nan. Is that smoke? Do you think it's a forest fire?"

Nancy looked away from the road long enough to see what Bess was talking about. "Oh no. I don't believe it."

"What?" George leaned forward from the backseat. "What are you talking about?"

"Fog." Nancy pointed to the thick white mist sliding between the trees and slipping down the side of the fern-covered hill. "Let's hope it's just a patch that we can get through in a hurry."

By the time they'd topped the ridge, then made their way down the other side in first gear, the fog was so thick that their headlights couldn't penetrate more than a few feet in front of them.

"All I can do is follow the line in the center of the road and just keep creeping along until the fog clears." Nancy clenched the wheel, her voice heavy with frustration.

All three sat on the edge of their seats, as if peering hard into the blinding white mist would help get them through it faster.

Nancy was not able to drive the jeep faster than ten, sometimes fifteen, miles an hour. Other cars came at them on the other side of the road, crawling along equally slowly, their headlights blurred halos.

"Maybe they'll cancel the climbing class,"

Bess said hopefully. "I mean they wouldn't go rock climbing in this stuff, would they?"

"Devil's Rock is a lot higher than this ground fog." She paused. "Wait a second, I think it's lifting now."

"You're right," George said, brightening. "And, look, there's a car without any headlights on. We must be nearly out—" She abruptly stopped talking as the jeep slid suddenly out of the fog. Ahead of them the road lay clear, the sun bright overhead.

"All right!" the three chorused at once.

"Let's move it!" Nancy called as she clamped her foot down hard on the gas pedal.

Bess didn't even shut her eyes when Nancy took the bends around the cliffs of the coast road at high speed. She was as eager as the other two to get there.

"I just hope we've made it in time," Nancy called out as she slammed the jeep to a halt in front of the main building several minutes later. Leaping out, she raced toward the front door.

"Tell me," she asked the girl at the front desk, "has the rock-climbing class left for Devil's Rock?"

"I'm sorry, Ms. Drew." The girl looked up casually from the romance novel she was reading. "But, yes, they've already left. But you're not able to take that class, anyway. It's advanced—"

"You don't understand," Nancy broke in firmly. "And I don't have time to explain. Just tell me, how long ago did they leave?"

"Nancy, hi." Gil's voice reached her ears as she felt him touch her arm. From the tense set of Nancy's face, he must have been able to tell something was wrong. "Marva?" he asked with slight dread. "Has something happened to her?"

"Not yet—I hope," Nancy replied, purposefully controlling her tone. "But we've got to hurry to prevent something from happening to her." Taking his arm, she pulled him, running and filling him in at the same time.

"And I think he intends to kill her at the same place where he murdered his partner," she finished at the jeep. "Is there a way to get up there, other than the hiking trail? A way I could drive the jeep?"

"I don't know—" Gil scowled. "Yes, I do remember. There's an old fire road that goes up the back of Devil's Rock, but I don't know what shape it's in. It might be overgrown—" He stopped. "What are we waiting for? Let's get going!"

"You'd better stay and show the police how to find that fire road." She pulled open the door and hopped in.

Bess and George were sitting inside, waiting for her. Nancy turned the key and ground it into gear as Gil gave her directions. A few seconds later they spun out, heading for Devil's Rock.

Gil was right, she thought as she reached the fire road. There was barely any resemblance to a real road left—just the bare bones of one as it wound up the steep, rocky hill. Nancy shifted into first and kept her foot steady on the gas. The thick brush was hood-high in several places. Still, they were making better time than if they'd tried to catch up with the class on foot.

They had nearly reached the top when George, who was leaning out the passenger side to guide Nancy, yelled a warning. "Watch out, Nancy. You're about to hit—"

Crunch! The sound of metal scraping and tearing was followed by silence as the jeep's engine sputtered and died.

"—a big rock," George finished lamely.

Nancy tried the ignition. Nothing. The jeep was out of commission. She paused long enough to consider the situation, then pulled on the hand brake and put the gearshift lever into first, so the jeep wouldn't roll back down the road. Leaping out, she started at a run up the final stretch, George and Bess right behind her.

The sight that greeted Nancy as she reached the top sent adrenaline shooting through her.

Marva was about to rappel, or climb down, over the side of the cliff.

"Marva, stop!" Nancy screamed as loud as she could. Half-running, half-flying, Nancy dove toward Marva, grabbing for her.

She managed to get ahold of Marva's hips and pull her back to the safety of solid ground.

With a surprised grunt, Marva wrestled herself free from Nancy's protective hold. "Nancy, what's wrong? Have you gone crazy?"

It was then that Nancy spotted the crucial instrument of Al's plan. She saw that Marva's carabiner—the metal ring used to hold her safety rope—had been filed nearly in two. If Marva had attempted to rappel down the face of Devil's Rock, the carabiner would have snapped under her weight. Marva would have fallen to her death.

Before she could point that out to Marva, Nancy saw Al rush at her. Hunt knocked Nancy to the ground hard. As she gasped for breath Nancy saw him slip a safety line around his waist. A second one hung around his neck.

In front of Nancy's horrified eyes, Al grabbed Marva. Before she had time to react, he pulled her rope off and slipped the second rope over Marva's head and down to her waist, cinching it tight. Dragging the frightened Marva with him, he headed for the edge.

"He's going to kill her!" Bess yelled in terror.

They watched, frozen, as the crazed man plunged headfirst over the face of Devil's Rock, taking Marva with him.

Chapter
Sixteen

WITH BESS'S SCREAM still echoing in her ears, Nancy pulled herself to her feet and rushed to the side of the cliff to look over.

Seventy or eighty feet below her, she could see Marva struggling with Al Hunt. They were locked together on one of the wide rock ledges that formed the devil's face.

As she watched the two figures scuffling below her, Nancy knew what the desperate killer was considering next.

Al Hunt had jerked Marva's safety rope back over her head and was trying to wrestle the young woman to the edge. Nancy had to get down there before he succeeded in pushing Marva to her death.

Nancy caught sight of the first safety rope that had been around Marva's waist and now hung free. It was bouncing against the cliff face. The rope still had to be secured to something at the top, Nancy thought. Yes, there it was, anchored securely to a large, solid boulder. Maybe she could rappel down to Marva.

Turning to the group of students who were now clustered at the edge watching the scene below with horrified fascination, Nancy took control. "Can someone show me how to use this rope to get down to that ledge?"

At first no one answered. The ones who had heard her just stared at her as if she were crazy. A slender boy of about seventeen finally answered her. "Look, if you have to ask us, you don't have any business trying to rappel down any cliff."

"Jerry's right. You'd only kill yourself doing it," a girl behind the boy spoke up.

Just then, another boy—one of those who'd never taken their eyes off what was happening below—yelled out, "Did you see that? Old man Hunt has really flipped out. Someone's got to save Ms. Phillips before she's history."

Nancy was feeling desperate. I've got to *do* something, she said to herself. I can't just stand here and let Marva die.

"Maybe if someone ran for help," the boy named Jerry suggested. "I could do it. I'm in track at school."

"There isn't time for that," Nancy blurted out. "We've got only seconds, at best."

"Nancy! Look!" A yell from George got her attention. "Up there!" George was pointing overhead. "Maybe that's help."

Bending her head back, Nancy shielded her eyes to look up in the direction George was pointing. Not far above, one of the club's hang gliders was circling the rock.

"It's Gil!" Bess said excitedly. "He's come to rescue Marva." She waved up at the hang-glider pilot. "Way to go, Gil!" she called.

Nancy held her breath as she watched Gil expertly manipulate the glider. Nancy guessed what Gil had in mind. He was going to attempt a landing on the ledge!

All the others were watching now, riveted to the colorful glider. A sudden flash of light from the ledge below made Nancy look down. With a sinking feeling of horror, she realized the flash had been the sun's reflection off the barrel of a gun. A gun Al Hunt had leveled at Gil.

Helplessly, Nancy watched as the killer fired once, then fired again. The first shot must have missed Gil. But the second one found its target. A small patch of red appeared on Gil's right shoulder. Gil flinched, and his hands jerked on the control bar. The glider's nose shot up too sharply, and it lost the lift—the crucial pressure of the wind under the sail— needed to keep it aloft. The sail began to flap dangerously.

A girl beside Nancy screamed. "Ohhhh— no!" Gil's body had sagged into his harness, his head drooping to one side. It looked as if he was losing consciousness.

"He's going to crash," Jerry said with a sharp intake of breath.

Just as it seemed Gil was going to take a dive, a sudden gust of wind caught the underside of the huge sail, billowing it up. The glider evened out on its own. Another gust sent the glider toward the top of Devil's Rock, in the direction of Nancy and the others.

"Catch it!" Nancy yelled as she ran to the center of the ledge. They had to intercept the runaway glider—it was their only hope!

Nancy's action triggered Jerry and George to run with her. They caught up with the glider and its unconscious pilot as it was about to sail on past them. Jumping easily, they grabbed the glider's frame and pulled it to them.

Down below Marva had managed to wedge herself between a large boulder and the cliff face. Having lost all connection with reality, Al Hunt was rocking the boulder back and forth like a man possessed. Soon he would reach his prize.

"Now what?" George asked as she helped

her friend unhook Gil's harness and ease the injured man to the ground. Bess knelt beside him, tearing away his shirt to examine the wound.

"I guess it's up to me now," Nancy replied. "Gil did say I was a natural at this sport. It's as good a time as any to find out if he was right."

"Nancy, no!" George implored. "Please don't do this—you've never taken one up before. You could make a fatal mistake!"

"I'll try not to," Nancy answered grimly. "Now help me turn this thing around so it's facing the edge."

"But what about the harness?" George asked. "Don't you need that? I'll get it off Gil."

"There isn't time," Nancy said as she and George, with the help of the two boys, lifted the glider and turned it. "I don't need the harness to fly. It's only a fancy safety belt." She gestured at the control bar—a triangular piece of aluminum tubing that was nearly five feet high at the center. "I'm going to stand on the base. I'll use my feet to push it back and forth, instead of my hands."

"You're crazy," George told her simply. "But I guess nothing I say is going to stop you."

"Right," Nancy said to her friend. "Wish me luck." Hefting the glider, Nancy ran toward the edge of the cliff and jumped off, swinging her feet up onto the crossbar sail and sending her soaring out over the valley.

Nancy had to crouch slightly because she was taller than the top of the tubular triangle. She used the weight of her body to bank the glider so she could head back toward the face of the huge rock.

Peering down at the ledge, what she saw made her cringe inside. Al Hunt had now caught sight of her. His arm was raised, and he had her dead in his gunsight.

Determined that she was not going to give him the chance to get off a good shot, Nancy went straight for the attack.

Aiming the glider at the ledge, she pushed the nose down. Diving straight for the burly climbing instructor, she tried to make her body as small a target as possible by crouching very low.

Marva, who had been momentarily forgotten by Hunt, saw her coming. As Hunt's attention was drawn to Nancy, Marva kicked out at his gun. She managed to knock it from his hand, where it hit the ledge and slithered across the slick granite out of his reach.

Good move, Marva, Nancy said to herself. Swiftly taking advantage of the situation, she raised herself up, then pushed the control bar forward as hard as she could. The glider's nose lifted and went into stall.

Its colorful sail flapping in protest, the glider descended, with a jolt, onto the ledge.

But the ledge wasn't wide enough for the glider, Nancy realized in horror. Slowly it began to inch backward, Nancy with it. Both would plunge to the valley floor, hundreds of feet below.

Bending her knees, Nancy sprung forward, as the glider began its final dizzy descent, and landed almost directly on top of the astonished Hunt. Before he could recover his balance, Nancy aimed a high karate kick at his jaw. Hunt went over backward, striking his head against a boulder. He lay still, his eyes closed.

"Is he—" Marva asked, slipping out of her hiding place.

"Dead?" Nancy bent over the man, feeling for his pulse at the base of his jaw. She looked up at Marva. "Just out cold. He'll be around to stand trial."

"Oh, Nancy!" Marva shuddered a sigh of relief. "I don't even know how to begin to thank you. You saved my life."

"Well, I can think of one way," Nancy replied with a glance at Al Hunt. "Help figure out how to get us down from here before he comes to."

Then Nancy heard a very welcome sound. Police sirens were echoing off the mountains around them. They really would be safe now.

Chapter

Seventeen

That was a pretty foolish thing you pulled, miss," the young detective said to Nancy. But his eyes expressed his admiration. "I don't think I'd be ready to launch myself into space —with only one lesson, you said?"

"I'm sure you do more dangerous things than that all the time," Nancy replied graciously. "I'm glad it's over."

"So am I." Marva breathed happily. "I'm happy to be down and away from that man." Her glance took in Al Hunt as he was being led away. "This time I hope he's locked up for good."

Hunt halted and turned to face the girls

when he heard Marva talking about him. His eyes were unfocused and wild looking. Nancy thought to herself, the man really is crazy— just as Bess had suggested the criminal behind these terrible acts must be.

"If it wasn't for you, Miss Private Snoop," Hunt spat, "no one would have guessed it was me who was sending those death threats—and setting up all those nice little accidents." His face cracked in an evil grin. "I should have hung you up with the frozen meat when I had the chance."

"How—how could you have pretended to be my friend when all the time you hated me?" Marva asked, bewildered by the change in the man she had considered almost as close as a real uncle.

"Easy." The mirthless grin was replaced by a snarl. "It was because I did hate you so much, and still *do*. You were a horrible little brat who sent me away to rot in jail." His eyes narrowed into slits. "But it gave me a lot of time to think up my revenge. And I almost succeeded this time—next time . . ."

"Come on, you!" The officer pulled on Hunt's arm. "You've done enough to this lady. You can shut up now."

As Marva and Nancy watched, the man who'd brought terror to Club High Adventure was led to a waiting squad car.

* * *

"You know, I still can't put the two men together in my mind," Marva said later that evening when they had all gathered in the lounge to discuss the case. "I can't believe that the awful man at the trial when I was a little girl is the same man I knew and counted on as a friend for the past three years since my dad died."

"That was the whole idea," Nancy said. She stretched her arms and legs, feeling relaxed now that the case was closed. "The death threats and accidents to the other guests were only meant to confuse things so no one would suspect you were the intended victim. I can't say for certain, but I don't think he honestly meant for the accidents to the guests to be deadly."

"How about Quinn?" George asked. "I mean, sure, we heard that he came out of his coma this afternoon. But he could have just as easily died."

"I still think that trap was meant for Marva," Nancy replied. "That trail's not for lone guests. He shouldn't have been there at all. So it was a matter of his being in the wrong place at the right time."

"And poor Lisa," Bess commented. "She's such a mixed-up kid. It probably didn't help that we all thought she sabotaged her own glider."

"Well, I believe she's going to be fine,"

Marva said, surprising them with her confident tone. "We had a little talk. She admitted that her father's sending her here was a good idea. I think it's helping her get over that boyfriend. And she's ready to go back and try to work things out with her father."

"Oh, I'm glad about that," Bess said. "I really like her."

"You know, it's funny," Marva mused. "I kept thinking that it was someone who was trying to ruin me so I'd sell the club."

Gil, who was sitting beside her, his arm in a sling to protect his injured shoulder, looked guilty when Marva said that. "I'm really sorry I ever tried to convince you to sell," he said. "I know you love the club. And I'll remember that from now on. I promise."

"I admit that's what threw me off at first," Nancy said. "I thought it was someone trying to scare you into selling as well. I was positive that was the motive. It was only after we found that partially burned photo that I realized I'd been on the wrong track all along. That's when I decided the motive was personal."

"And since the photo was found in Al Hunt's cabin . . ." George shrugged expressively.

"It had to be him," Bess finished.

"Well, I'm just glad the club's reputation is

safe now," Marva said happily, and snuggled up closer to Gil.

"Yeah," Gil said, dropping a kiss on the top of her head. "I'm glad, too. After everything that happened this afternoon, I realized I've come to think of the club as home. I just might even end up loving it as much as Marva."

"Well, you'd better," Marva said jokingly, and kissed Gil back. "After all, we're going to be spending the rest of our lives here." She turned to Nancy. "Gil mentioned this afternoon that it would be nice if we ran it as a married couple. So I'll be exchanging this engagement ring for a wedding band. And he'll be exchanging all his other girls for just one—me."

"Marva, how wonderful," Bess exclaimed. "When?"

"Soon," Gil said. "The sooner, the better." He squeezed Marva's hand. "Then we're going on a nice long honeymoon. I think we could do with a vacation."

"Oh, that's funny." Bess giggled. "A vacation from a vacation resort."

After the collective groans had died down, Marva asked, "But how about you three? Can you steal a few days before you go back to River Heights?"

At Nancy's nod, she invited them. "Then please spend it here at the club as my—our—guests," she said with a quick grin at Gil.

"You'll get to know the club for the wonderful place it really is."

Nancy and George exchanged delighted glances. Despite Bess's small moan of protest, they agreed that Club High Adventure could be the perfect place to spend a few restful days.

Nancy's next case:

Handsome deejay Jon Villiers is the hottest thing in town. All the girls who crowd the trendy new club Moves are crazy about him. But Jon has eyes only for Laurie Weaver, and quite a few people—including Laurie's ex-boyfriend—don't like the idea.

One of them is intent on breaking up the romance the hard way. When a series of mysterious accidents threatens Laurie, Nancy steps in. The teen sleuth discovers that sexy Jon has a shady past and an unsavory present. If Nancy doesn't crack the case fast, her own future may be on its last legs . . . in *LAST DANCE*, Case #37 in The Nancy Drew Files™.

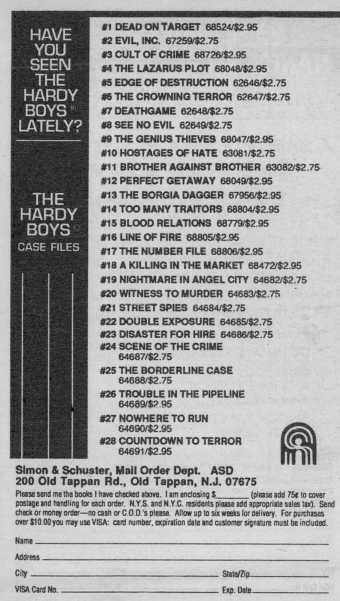